Category: Dedalus Europe
General Editor: Timothy Lan

Take Six:
Six Estonian
Women Writers

Take Six:
Six Estonian
Women Writers

edited by Elle-Mari Talivee

translated by Slade Carter

Dedalus

Dedalus would like to thank the Traducta Programme of the Cultural Endowment of Estonia and Arts Council, England in London for their assistance in producing this book.

Supported using public funding by
ARTS COUNCIL
ENGLAND

CULTURAL ENDOWMENT of ESTONIA

Published in the UK by Dedalus Limited
24-26, St Judith's Lane, Sawtry, Cambs, PE28 5XE
info@dedalusbooks.com
www.dedalusbooks.com

ISBN printed book   978 1 915568 77 9
ISBN ebook   978 1 915568 90 8

Dedalus is distributed in the USA & Canada by SCB Distributors
15608 South New Century Drive, Gardena, CA 90248
info@scbdistributors.com   www.scbdistributors.com

Dedalus is distributed in Australia by Peribo Pty Ltd
58, Beaumont Road, Mount Kuring-gai, N.S.W. 2080
info@peribo.com.au   www.peribo.com.au

First published by Dedalus in 2025
Foreword and Selection copyright © Elle-Mari Talivee 2025
Translation and Notes copyright © Slade Carter 2025
Texts which are in copyright are copyright their individual authors.

The right of Elle-Mari Talivee to be identified as the editor and Slade Carter as the translator of this work has been asserted by them in accordance with the Copyright, Designs and Patents Act, 1988.

Printed and bound in the UK by Clays Elcograf S.p.A.
Typeset by Marie Lane

A C.I.P. listing for this book is available on request.

The Editor

Elle-Mari Talivee, PhD, is a scholar, critic and essayist. She divides her time between her roles as a literary adviser at the Estonian Literature Centre and as a researcher at the Museum of the Under and Tuglas Literature Centre of the Estonian Academy of Sciences in Tallinn.

She has edited two books for Dedalus: *Baltic Belles* (*The Dedalus Book of Estonian Women's Literature*) and *Take Six: Six Estonian Women Writers*.

The Translator

Slade Carter was born in Australia but has long made his home in London. He studied at the University of Melbourne, Imperial College London, and the University of Tartu.

His first novel, a children's fantasy adventure, *The Helios Book*, was published in 2024. He translates from Estonian, and his translations include short stories, book chapters, author profiles, and Ene Sepp's young adult novel *Sorry, say that again?! (Vabandust, aga mis asja?!)*

He lives in London with his wife and two children.

Contents

Foreword:
The compelling voices of
Estonian women writers

Spring arrives in Estonia in March, which is also the month for literary awards. The most important Estonian short story prize, the Tuglas Short Story Award, is presented annually on 2nd March to the two best writers of the previous year. Friedebert Tuglas (1886-1971) was a classic Estonian author, who in addition to writing unparalleled short forms, promulgated a structure for the short story in Estonian literature—each genuine short story must have a compact plot, few characters, one central theme, and a twist at the end: perhaps the short story is a sonnet in prose. Tuglas established the prize in his will. The 2nd March was the birthday of the literary master, and so he gave a kind of birthday present to the short story virtuosos of the future.

In Estonia, snow is often still on the ground in March, but the fragrance of spring is in the air—thaw!—and a short story that is sensitive and structured on the one hand, and on the other, a very experimental literary genre seems just right in the early spring of Northern countries. The short story is a genre that can be as unpredictable as spring weather by the Baltic Sea.

All the women authors selected for this collection possess the Tuglas Short Story Award in their prize cabinet, although the winning story is not necessarily represented in this selection. Diving into the overall statistics of the winners brings us directly to Virginia Woolf's challenge. Woolf found in her essay *'A Room of One's Own'* that "A woman must have money and a room of her own if she is to write fiction."

As of 2025, the Tuglas prize has been awarded fifty-five times, thirty-four of which have been bestowed on men, even though the Estonian women's short story has been considered strong throughout the award's existence. An exception to the early decades of the prize occurred in 1983, when the prize was awarded to Aino Pervik and Asta Põldmäe. The second decade of this century signifies a marked change: more often than not, one of the laureates is a man, the other a woman. However, in 2024 and 2025, the award was only given to women writers.

There are more women writing today, including short story genre enthusiasts—which is reflected in the annual Estonian short story collections—which must mean that women finally have more time and opportunity to write. Perhaps at last they have room(s) in which to write. The Estonian short story is currently crowned by the sensitive and special pen of women, where women's experience is often voiced. The list of laureates over the years also indicates that the next move after the short story is often a longer work of prose, in which the increasingly powerful, very appealing voice of women writers is also manifest in Estonia. All the authors in this collection have written at least one novel, except the youngest, Aliis Aalmann, who has excelled with her first short stories. All of the selected authors have tried their hand in several genres, such as writing for children, poetry, translating or finding expression in fields other than fiction—for example, art.

The collection opens with Aino Pervik's short story, *'The Moment of Ornamentation'*. This is a tale of a mother of three children trying to imagine, with longing and worry, what might happen to her dear family members while they are away in a foreign land. She is a textile artist and her husband has travelled to Siberia for an expedition to the Khanty indigenous people, taking along their barely adult student daughter. The artist sets up camp on an islet in order to draw, and her partly irrational concern for her family's wellbeing culminates in a preternatural ending. However, in Pervik's short story *'Anna'*, visions unfold in an exhausted, fevered night, a representation of the supernatural qualities often attributed to women, including knowledge of witchcraft, qualities that are feared and hated. Perhaps the author is also questioning the nature of suffocating love.

This collection presents an outstanding opportunity to publish a mother's and daughter's stories side by side. Piret Raud is the youngest of Aino Pervik's three children (who have all written books) with her husband, the writer Eno Raud. Piret Raud is an artist who first began writing for children but has increasingly turned to the adult reader and published short stories and novels. Her short prose is very metaphorical, with unexpected twists. Both stories in this collection represent a model structure of short story denouement. *'The Bench'* also illustrates how Piret Raud's artistic creation sometimes fuses the living and the inanimate, things and creatures do not have distinct boundaries, but form or blur where we least expect it. Raud's work has sometimes been classified as magical realism. The short story *'The Paper Bird'* with its surprising ending, conveys the daily life of an elderly woman who is looking for the means to becalm her still passionate emotional life.

Kätlin Kaldmaa is probably the most restlessly international of the authors in this book: she feels at home not only in Estonia, but also in Iceland and Greece. In her witty and sarcastic way, she blurs the borders between Estonia and the rest of the world. In *'Shitty Story'*, the protagonist is a contemporary career woman who describes a long business trip abroad that is complicated by gastrointestinal issues. The protagonist can deal with almost any problem by combining black humour with feminine practicality. The wonderfully poetic short prose piece *'When the Boys came'*, however, conveys the singular seismic turmoil when child-ren—daughters—grow into adulthood, and the unexpected silence when the children have suddenly left home. Kaldmaa has also portrayed the complex process of growing up as a young person, especially the complicated emotions of a young girl. Together with her daughter Hanneleele Kaldmaa, the writer walked the pilgrimage of Camino de Santiago, resulting in a jointly written travel book, *Kaks armastuslugu* (Two Love Stories, 2017), which deals with the relationships between mothers and daughters over several generations.

The tale of the protagonist in Mudlum's short story *'My Aunt Ellen'* can be summed up as the life story of a famous man's wife. The author however, has turned that point of view upside down. Aunt Ellen may have had a famous husband, but the real treasure is herself. She has a fairy-tale house and garden, and the ability to share all of this with her young relatives, teaching them to notice the wonderful minutiae of everyday life and to create fairy tales themselves. Even when Aunt Ellen's life starts to be overshadowed by mental illness, there are moments of light that shine like pearls on her clear days. This short story is characteristic of Mudlum in conveying the relationship between surroundings and objects: the author trained as a fashion designer, she can make beautiful things, but also possesses the gift of describing everything in such a way that the reader has a sense of feeling a fabric or beautiful thing between their fingers. Another example of Mudlum's short prose, *'The Women's Sauna'* exemplifies contemporary traits of the Estonian short story. Complying with a fastidious structure is not especially important, and the short prose text is a slice of someone's thoughts or memories—the short story depicts a childhood memory of the Estonian city dweller's sauna experience. In the communal sauna, women congregate in the hellish heat, and with the help of soap and whisks, thoroughly cleanse themselves inside and out, and share the wisdom of women with one another. The sauna has played an important role in Estonian traditional culture: it was used in marriage proposals and wedding customs, for giving birth, healing the sick and even death. Even now, it seems impossible for Estonians to cope for a long time without a sauna. They are keen to share their sauna experiences, even with those who are barely known to them, this rite of passage and ritual of purification or trial. In 2023, Estonian director Anna Hints' film *Smoke Sauna Sisterhood* was released, winning the Best

Documentary Award at the European Film Awards. In some senses, the film has parallels to Mudlum's story.

Lilli Luuk's story *'The Boys in the Snow'* takes the reader back to Estonia in the late 1980s, during the period of Soviet occupation. The period alludes to the Chornobyl (Chernobyl) disaster in Ukraine in 1986, which included Estonians among the 'liquidators' tasked with dealing with the consequences of the incident. In this short story, the father of a family has just returned from there and has decided to have no further contact with his family because of the danger of radiation. The mother is left alone with their two boys, working as a veterinarian, her heart further weighed down by anxiety about her elder son, who is conscripted into the Soviet army. Young men from the Baltic States often returned from the Russian army as cripples or in a tin coffin, as a result of accidents caused by indifference, or the torture of young soldiers, or as a consequence of hazing and abuse (called *dedovshchina* in Russian) either murdered or committing suicide. In 1979, the Soviet Union invaded Afghanistan and waged a ten-year war. Over one and a half thousand young men from tiny Estonia were sent to Afghanistan. Thirty-six of these died, while many of those who returned brought the trauma of war home with them. Lilli Luuk's short story also reflects the fear and despair of the mothers, sisters, and brides of these soldier boys. This story is presented through a second lens, the eyes of the younger brother: the younger son of the family is left alone with his own worries and can no longer cope with the violence at school. By contrast, the short story *'Life, like in a Film'* is not necessarily linked to a specific place or time, although it does contain references to similar events. The story centres on a family who, after a tragic accident, have developed addiction problems, where the children grow up in a similar pattern of life from which escape seems impossible. In addition to the narrative, the backbone of the short story is the filmography of that time. The narrator looks at the events of her life with bitter irony, like scenes from famous films, which may be analogous in every country.

Aliis Aalmann has made a powerful debut in Estonian literature: in the years 2021-2024, she received three prestigious poetry and prose prizes. Aliis Aalmann is a teacher in the small town of Võru in southern Estonia, and she also works as an artist. The long and poetic story *'I still didn't go to School then'* has twice garnered awards. In addition to the Tuglas Award, it also won the prize of the Estonian 101-year-old literary magazine *Looming* ('Creation'). The story conveys the world through the eyes of a little girl. She has recently lost her brother, and in the company of adults, older children, and pets, she is seeking an explanation for her feelings, a way to understand what has happened, and a way to grieve. In Aalmann's second story in this collection, *'To the Moon'*, a rather simple man tries with all his soul to win the heart of his female neighbour.

This collection of short stories offers a varied expedition into great Estonian short prose on the one hand, and on the other, a journey into Estonian life, customs and history. The world is seen here mostly through the eyes of a woman from North-East Europe. In the spring of 2024, Maarja Kangro, also a prize-winning author, was elected to lead the Estonian Writers' Union. She noted in her post-election interview how important it is for women to see that their voice is heard.

The Authors

Aino Pervik (born 1932) is one of Estonia's best-loved children's authors. She has published over 60 children's books, which have been translated into many languages and made into animated and live-action films. After graduating from a teaching institute, and from there the Finno-Ugric language department at the University of Tartu, Aino Pervik worked as an editor in publishing and television, and translated Hungarian literature into Estonian. A freelance writer since 1967, she became a member of the Writers' Union in 1974. For adults, she has written two collections of short stories, four novels and poetry collections, travelogues, critiques, and memoires in the form of the wonderful *Miniatuurid mälupõhjast* ('Miniatures from the Depths of Memory,' 2020), which have also been published in Hungarian.

Friedebert Tuglas Short Story Award, 1983.

The Authors

Piret Raud (born 1971) is a graduate of the Estonian Academy of Arts with a master's degree in graphic art. In addition to illustrating children's books, the freelance artist began to write them herself, and her children's books have been translated into many of the world's languages. Since 2006, Piret Raud has been a member of the Estonian Writers' Union. Raud started writing for adults quite recently—her first novel was published in 2018. To date, she has published four novels—the last was *Keedetud hirvede aeg* ('The Age of Boiled Deer,' 2024)—and two collections of short fiction, and her short story selections have also been translated into Polish and Hungarian.

Friedebert Tuglas Short Story Award, 2022.

Kätlin Kaldmaa (born 1970) studied Estonian and English language and literature and semiotics at the University of Tartu and has worked in journalism, publishing and children's literature. She has been the head of the Estonian PEN Club and the International Secretary of PEN International. The author, who began her writing career as a poet, is now a freelancer. Since 2008 she has been a member of the Estonian Writers' Union. As a translator, Kaldmaa has translated fiction from English, Spanish and Finnish. Kaldmaa has regularly transferred the experimental language of poetry to prose. Kaldmaa's first novel *Islandil ei ole liblikaid* ('No Butterflies in Iceland') was published in 2013, and there are now two short story collections, selections of which have appeared in Hungarian and Finnish.

Friedebert Tuglas Short Story Award, 2012.

The Authors

Mudlum (born 1966) is a writer and literary critic. She lives in Tallinn and on the small Estonian island of Muhu. She studied Estonian literature, theatre studies and philosophy at the Estonian Institute of Humanities and graduated from the Estonian Academy of Arts. Mudlum became a writer through her association with the literary group ZA/UM, and initially wrote stories for the group's blog. Mudlum has published collections of short stories and essays, four novels, and children's books. She has been a member of the Estonian Writers' Union since 2017. Two of her novels have been awarded the Estonian Cultural Endowment's Award for Prose, and her novel *Poola poisid* ('Polish Boys,' 2019) also won the European Union Prize for Literature. Friedebert Tuglas Short Story Award, 2017.

Lilli Luuk (born 1976) won the Tuglas Short Story Award for her literary debut/short story 'The Hole.' She has now won two of these awards, and her short stories have been recognised by the literary magazine *Looming* with its annual award. The author is an art historian by education (University of Tartu), who has worked as a teacher and lecturer. As an artist, she has performed at art exhibitions. Since 2021, Lilli Luuk has been a freelance writer. She has published a collection of short stories and two novels. Her last novel *Ööema* ('Night Mother,' 2024), has been awarded several literary awards in 2025, including the State Annual Cultural Award. A member of the Estonian Writers' Union since 2023, when Lilli Luuk was also chosen as the Estonian Writer of the Year. Friedebert Tuglas Short Story Award, 2018 and 2021.

The Authors

Aliis Aalmann (born 1995) has not yet published a novel, but her first collection of poems, *Verihaljas* ('Blood Green' 2021), has received a debut prize in its year of publication, and her second collection of poems received acclaim. She has also performed her poems at poetry slams. Aliis Aalmann has a master's degree from the University of Tartu and teaches Estonian, literature and history in Võru, a small town in South Estonia, where she is also active in the field of art. Her poetry is meditative and multilayered. The same contours are conveyed in the dramatic plots of her short stories, where her experiments in the genre have also won notable recognition.

Friedebert Tuglas Short Story Award, 2024.

The Moment of Ornamentation

Aino Pervik

Water splashing under the oars, Milvi could not row very quietly. It was a miracle she could manage at all. Herman shouted something to her from the shore. No doubt he gave good advice, but the burbling water and the creak of the oarlocks combined with bird shrieks to mask his words. Milvi had no appetite to hear what Herman had to say to her. She was already straining with all her might and focus to keep the boat moving more or less in a straight line. The main thing was that Herman let her carry on. Now, no matter what Herman shouted, he wouldn't come after her in the motorboat.

The open water was filled with the sounds of the sea. The

water was clear to the bottom, with dark algal rocks and light gravel visible below. It was strange to feel that heightened clarity carrying her aloft. Gradually, the bottom slipped deeper away, becoming greener and darker. An unevenly curving, jagged line trailed behind the boat. Milvi slowly calmed down, joy swelled inside her. One could still have noticed and recognised her from the shore, but they don't come to the sea so early in the morning. And Herman won't tell. They will know that Milvi went elsewhere, and will not think about her until it's time to be someplace else.

There was a rolled-up tent and rucksack in the stern of the boat. The pack held things for overnighting and watercolour supplies. Milvi wanted to try the watercolours again. She could already sense some of the light opening up in every direction, on which silence hangs with the sounds of the sea. She knew what she was going to do. She has several days to act, without offending anyone with her aloof disposition, without disturbing anyone with distractions. Only with discretion. There was no need to pack several days' worth of hearty breakfasts, lavish lunches or perfect dinners accompanied by aperitifs, cocktails and shots, for several days you are not required to follow a conversation that keeps moving along the shortest dotted line in a clear triangular schema of income, acquisition, and consumption. She is not eating anything today. She won't eat, nor does she give any idea about why she does not eat. Today she will break the law of nature and create the world.

Milvi was ready to show her world to a willing observer, one who is ready to follow the signs that she has placed, without ripping them out and angrily relocating them. The relocations will still come out wrong, because it is hard to perceive Milvi's world when one is anxious and angry, and anger grows when misplaced signs do not get to where the angry set their sights. Yet the blame falls on Milvi.

Milvi wove her own rugs, printed fabrics and towels, took pictures for strangers who approached her. The approaching person is invited, because without them everything remains stuffy and closed, the one who reaches out is as necessary as air. Yet a professional artist must also accept the fact that their work is viewed as compulsive. Coercion is not created by the artist, but by the artist's bread. The one who pays is no longer the spectator, but the owner, and so art becomes compulsive for the payer. The compulsive spectator, in defiance of compulsion, tries to throw the stunted truth into the lungs of the creator, to allow the creator to breathe for that singular moment. In this way, he or she hopes to become an enforcer too. Public success can protect against the compulsive observer because success can calm the spectator. However, there are also those who cannot tolerate artistic success.

Milvi was quite successful.

Her shoulders and back were already sore from rowing. To Milvi, it seemed as if the seabed was level with the ground and was not deepening. With the tide mark visible on the surface of the water, with each heavy stroke of the oar it felt as though the boat was gliding higher and higher into the open sky.

Dense reddish reeds with spotted verdant rushes grew on the edge of the landward side of the islet of Rihka. This stretch was accessed from the seaward side by a long rocky cape that could not be seen at high tide. Rihka was Milvi and Väino's long-established childhood island. Every summer, when aunt Salme, uncle Gunnar and Vambola visited them, they went there on two boats to feast among the junipers and rocks. The meal consisted of fried herring, boiled eggs, spring onions and bread. The drink was taken from nature, bringing special joy to the children: a tiny well was dug in the gravel, from which clear cold water could be drawn after only half an hour. During the war, there were no outings, later there was no boat. Aunt Salme and uncle Gunnar were no more. Neither were Mum and Dad. These days, trips were no longer made to Rihka, whose beach was visible from the shore, now there are journeys to more distant places. These days, excursions were by motorboat, a bottle of vodka in the bottom of the vessel.

Milvi slid her craft over the rocks by the shore. The water was shallow, the boat was hard to shift. Still, she had to be dragged over the high waterline, for anyone who knows the sea, understands that when it rises, it will take hold of a little boat and endlessly rock it back and forth. Milvi got soaked from the exertion but managed to get the boat's upper rudder back behind the rushes. It may be that Milvi was unnecessarily cautious and wasted her efforts, but she had her heart set on the task, and she did not have to explain it to anyone.

Milvi then carried her things to the campsite among the stones and trees, took a small hiking shovel from her rucksack and immediately started digging a well. She could still remember the well site of her childhood. It was difficult to burrow into the gravel, but Milvi was not in a hurry. Eventually, the hole grew deep enough. Not quite with the same steep sides or face like those created by her father and Uncle Gunnar, but nonetheless the water began to seep into Milvi's well.

Setting up the tent was the easiest of the jobs, Milvi had the skills for that. The tent was too spacious for her alone;

previously Milvi and Sulev, together with their twin boys and little Kadri would fit snugly inside. Not any more. The twins were now all grown up, each with their own lives. Kadri had realised a long-held dream, she was a student of history. At this moment she was with Sulev on an expedition to Siberia. Every summer, Milvi was visiting her brother's family. Her childhood home was hospitable, but now her brother was spending the summer there with his wife Maret, their children and Maret's mother. The sauna, the kitchen, the barbecue, and the outdoor grill managed their needs completely, to fulfil their ideas of summer to the end.

Milvi unrolled the sleeping bag in the tent, took a towel and went to the sea. She tried to swim away from the lingering thoughts hanging over her, tried to focus only on observing the water, air and light. It didn't quite work out. The attitudes and meanings of recent days were all still sharp, they had to be dissolved piece by piece, word by word, into her own understandings and thoughts before peace could be attained.

The tension between Maret's brother and his wife was a sticky mass that drew others in. You could not be present without feeling breathless, being pulled in all possible directions. The teeth grinding of Maret's mother was particularly intolerable, so what if they didn't have a go at Milvi, but instead took a bite out of Liia. Unfortunately, Milvi was never immune to the hostility of strangers. She didn't fit in with the haters. Of course, she was overly sensitive, but what could she do since she was born with fragile nerves, and even later she had not tried to calm her sensitivities at all, so what if she got hurt. At home, Milvi is endlessly amenable. It did not bother her that some called her flexible stance a kind of oppression. Milvi felt that this approach was robust and was disturbed by the strong desire of others to undermine her position and impose their own. Milvi had room in her soul to move about. Sulev couldn't care less about trivial things either.

After swimming, Milvi warmed herself on a wide hot stone. She tried to coax the stone's peace into herself, tried to listen to the stone's world. The stone is still there, it will not move or leave there. The stone only knows the water that is there, this shore and the sun, the wind and the sky as they come to it. Milvi tried to think of herself as the stone. She had done this since childhood, imaging herself as a tree, a flower, a bush, someone standing still under the open sky. Thinking thus of herself in terms of plants or stones, Milvi perceived herself as an incomplete whole, where that which is missing does not irritate, depress or become bitter, but instead promises. Without the promise, Milvi would have dried up. That is why she couldn't eat too much over too long a period, because then heavy laziness and flabbiness came and took away alertness and perception, making living a torment. Of course, it was not appropriate to say this to Maret's sister-in-law or Maret's brother's family, much less Maret's mother. It would have been unusually offensive to them. Endless stupidity drives further anger. Milvi lacked the militancy to resist anger, she was far more vulnerable than those who stir up anger; anger alone paralysed her ability to respond, even words disappeared from her mouth.

The morning had grown into day and Milvi set up her easel. Small flies walked along her bare legs and shoulders, buzzing around her. They were annoying, but Milvi thought that, in fact, she is the intruder here, that she must know that before and after her presence this was empty, ungoverned space, and that neither she nor any other person can make sense of this little isle. This islet is independent of people and has its own goings on.

Milvi quickly got on with the task. She never had to struggle through a long period of procrastination before taking on work, her outer shell was so thin that she did not have to remove anything from it or dig herself out of it to prepare for work. Thus, she was more easily hurt by an outsider than one who, for the sake of creative work, had to make a great effort to progress from one situation to the next. Milvi was usually feeling vulnerable as soon as she got to work.

Right now, however, she was full of a special listening energy, it only came in nature, and that is why Milvi loved to work outdoors. She felt how, looking from the inside, her dimensions change, her body shrinks, while her ability to listen becomes more and more dominant, growing into a rift that stretches across an unknown territory, through which it contacts other life that lives beside it. Milvi did not analyse colours, did not separate them into nuances, nor look for hues. It was as if she had not been a selector of signs, the choice happened by itself, becoming clear before reaching her. She knew exactly how it had to be done, just as if there was a moment of crystallisation of the surrounding mystery into an image in the air, a moment of conjuring permanent contact, the only clear and pure path to follow. Thus, something that may not be obvious to her now, but that may be the closest thing to the key, could become apparent later. The image was merely a random form, the one in Milvi's power. Milvi worked quickly, this feeling of clarity and fluidity, where everything seemed to come from somewhere else, was comparable to the inception of madness, a state of being where insanity is present alongside a sharp mind, both rushing anxiously in the same direction, with the force of madness and a clear head.

Afterwards, Milvi was exhausted. She limped along the shore that shimmered in the hot blaze. From the reeds she moved up among the trees. Colossal, late strawberries grew there in the shade. No one had been here; the wild strawberries were super-ripe and untouched. Milvi ate them, and through the strawberries her thoughts turned to the children. She was worried about how Kadri would hold up on the expedition. Kadri was not exactly a robust and healthy girl. Of course, Sulev was there, but he had to work. They had gone to make a film about the Khanty. Sulev had been preparing for this film for several years, he had already been there last summer. Sulev also took Kadri's friend Riina along, as the girls wanted to do coursework on the ethnography of the Khanty people. If only they could manage it OK. Sometimes Kadri's periods were excruciatingly heavy, and she would lie in bed for a few days in pain. She wondered what Sulev was going to do with her there. Yet Kadri could not be stopped from going. Unfortunately, Kadri had to live inside her body and adjust her entire life to its limitations. So what if a spirit is awakened? The body has to endure.

In the afternoon, Milvi went to dig up northern bedstraw roots to use for dyeing some yarn. The smell of these yellow and whitish flowers represented one of the signs of summer heat for Milvi, the strong smell of bedstraw was always associated with dryness and heat, hot stones, dusty sand. On the islet, the plant was lush, and their roots were strong and sturdy. Milvi tied them together in bundles and hung them from a birch branch to dry in the wind. Some ancient roots had risen from the ground, white moss had grown around them, and they looked like trunks, yet in the form of a root that was writhing about, creating the impression of something sensitive yet strong and tenacious, with a keen sense of its surroundings and a powerful urge to preserve itself.

Milvi collected dry branches that had fallen from the birches, broke them apart and laid them in rows near the tent. She picked up a large log and lit a fire. Sulev's father had a soldier's billycan in his rucksack, in which they loved to make tea. This billycan was with Sulev's father throughout the war, it signified comfort during the war, a symbol of survival. Milvi's fingers sought contact with the essence of things, and this billycan was far from a sheet of tin stamped into a soulless, hollow vessel. However, its soul had come from somewhere else, not from the moulding or from the maker's hands. It was given life by Sulev's father's hope.

Milvi drew water from her crater-like well into the billy can and hung it over the fire. She had tea and sugar in a tin can, which she had put into her rucksack in the city, just in case, along with salt and pepper. She had taken a piece of bread and potatoes in a plastic bag from Maret's pantry. She did not start preparing the potatoes, she didn't need food yet, though she wanted tea. Milvi picked a handful of thyme, put it in a jug next to the tea leaves and poured it over the boiling water. Milvi loved to swathe tea with wild herbs, she needed not only to look, but also to feel the taste, smell, touch. The whole body, all the senses had to take part. That was Milvi's way.

Tea mug in hand, she began to look at her mid-morning

work. She did not see it from the outside yet, she was still inside. In a couple of places, she would have liked to be more precise, but she couldn't fix it any more. She would have to try it again.

Milvi put the picture away and took a handkerchief from her rucksack. While doing so, her hand landed on Sulev's comb. She had the same comb as Sulev, though each had a different colour: Milvi's was white, Sulev's black. They had been switched when Sulev went to Siberia. Sulev's comb had gone missing, and Milvi gave him hers. It turned out that Sulev had accidentally put the comb in Milvi's rucksack while he was packing. Milvi drew Sulev's comb through her hair. Her heart became heavy. The man suddenly seemed terribly vulnerable in his filmmaking, which was already taking place, and where lightning strikes your nerves before you even decide to step into the rain.

The anxiety suddenly felt overwhelming, and weakness spread over her body, her arms stopped tingling, her fingertips were stinging. Milvi tried to calm herself sensibly, why should she exorcise ghosts. Sulev had enough authority, he was firm and exacting. Yet lately he lost his temper easily, slept badly, and drank wine alone at night. Worry piled up around Milvi in an exaggerated abundance, threatening to come crashing down on her head. Milvi escaped into the water.

The sea was a restless pink grey. The water felt good, at length Milvi swam far from the shore, the gentleness of the sea smoothed away the nervous feeling layer by layer in thin crusts, until only softness remained.

The air seemed cool when Milvi finally came out of the water, and she lit another fire to warm herself. She made this fire a little away from the tent among the big rocks, because she did not want it to be visible to the sea. Milvi was afraid of being noticed. She could not be seen from inland, as the area was hidden by the trees on the island. The light was not visible from behind the rocks to the sea either. Only when it gets dark does light rise higher. Voices rang out and echoed all around, there was a distant barking of dogs, birds chirping nearby, a faint burbling, crackling, rustling. Milvi refrained from making noise, moved quietly and stealthily. Milvi's fear was not clear or explicable, what she was vaguely afraid of was the evil eye, a strange glance, the pressure of external desires.

In the deep darkness, Milvi woke up from a disturbing dream. She was hot inside her sleeping bag, sweat was pouring under her chin and between her breasts. The floor of the tent was wide and hard, Milvi could not immediately find a suitable position to fall asleep again, and now she was already wide awake. She would have liked to press herself against her sleeping children, to feel that there was more than one of her. Little Kadri usually lay next to Milvi in the tent, with the boys and Sulev on the other side of the tent partition. Now they were all gone, the tent was empty and silent.

Milvi felt scared. It was a childhood fear of ghosts. The fear was the same as a child's, but the ghosts that flickered outside had changed. The rattling skeleton man was no longer sitting in the darkness on a tree branch as before, instead icy girls walked without moving their legs across the broad rocks and trees, separating only when passing the tent on both sides. They had identical oval faces and long slithering bodies like algae. Milvi was not afraid of their nearness or their touch, nor of their strangling hands or the shredding champing of their ghostly teeth, as she had been afraid as a child. Milvi was horrified by those eyes, which held the rawness of despair and hopelessness. There, in the eyes of these girls and women, was the world's outpouring of anguish, ignorance, and anticipation of doom. The ghosts might not be fully formed, but their shape did not matter when despair was over water and land, as they both walked past Milvi that night like cold, elongated girls with colourless hair. Their human appearance made them more terrifying to Milvi than their ethereal state could have been.

Milvi curled up in her sleeping bag, into a voiceless human struggling to breathe, to keep from being overwhelmed by despair. Over long hours, she struggled half-asleep and listening to the fits and starts of ghostly incantations. Then it grew light outside, the ghosts were at peace, and so was Milvi.

Morning swimming can be considered a cleansing ritual. Milvi felt holy when she ate some bread while holding a hot mug of tea in her hand atop a stone in the sunshine. To accompany the bread, she ate the tender sorrel and yarrow leaves that grew in the shade, which she dipped in salt.

Today, Milvi wanted to draw the lush bird's-foot-trefoil that grows rampant in these parts. Milvi loved to use raw images drawn directly from nature on towels and fabrics, weaving ornamentation into rugs. There was something magical about the transformation of the image from nature into ornamentation, it was like catching a secret, holding the key. The defining moment comes when the form still exists in nature but is no more, having already become a symbol. It is a juncture where all meanings are still there and already exist. Milvi sensed a feeling of completely different lives at the moment of the ornamentation's creation, being human and something else at the same time, feeling the maddening hope of several different lives bursting inside herself at once. It wasn't something that could be kept inside. It was Milvi's duty to show this sign.

Milvi worked, flushed and sweating, until her hands were numb. She lay down in a place sheltered from the wind to sunbathe, to rest in the sun and warm her shivering body, which had become cold. The heat soon made her calm and sleepy. A sense of time disappeared, Milvi shifted to a zone of unconscious visions. Before her closed eyes, a slender black flower, shiny as tar, burst out from the sun into the reddish-grey softness, symmetrical and asymmetrical at the same time, erupting with sleek black stems and silky petals. The root emerged from deep below, it had not yet reached the blue sky, growing only through subterranean reds and yellows. Milvi was neither sleeping nor awake, the flower in front of her eyes floated between clarity and blur, the hum of a boat engine faintly reached her ears. It became increasingly clear that this sound of reality was rapidly approaching. Milvi suddenly became alert, her heart began to beat, a shock of fright made her sit up with a jolt. She looked at the sea. Nose up, stern in the water, a boat was quickly drawing near.

Milvi's first instinct was to hide like a lizard, but of course there was nowhere to go. She dressed quickly. Her hands were shaking, a weakness in her knees. From behind a boulder, she peeked out at the person approaching. The boat seemed to carry just one person. Maybe it's Herman, Milvi tried to reassure herself. Definitely Herman, he's come to see how Milvi is getting along. However, he was not at all like the lean Herman who dressed in dull clothes. The man in the boat was large and stocky and wore a bright blue sweatshirt.

Then Milvi recognised him.

It was Väino, her twin brother, how could she not have known him right away!

Why would Väino be coming here for her? How does he even know where to look for her? Herman promised to keep quiet.

Something has happened to the children or Sulev. In a flash, she felt anxiety that began to coldly and silently touch Milvi's trembling heart. Milvi rushed fearfully, feet flying, towards the boat. An accident, she thought. Sulev, Kadri, Mart, Madis. Väino guided the bobbing boat to the beach, stopped the engine and climbed over the vessel's side and into the water. He was wearing black fisherman's boots up to the groin, his big body swaying above them as he wordlessly pulled the boat toward the shore.

Milvi did not dare to ask. She stood and was silent, her eyes on Väino's gloomy face.

'Look, here you are,' said Väino from knee-deep water.

'Did something happen?' an almost voiceless question ruptured from Milvi when her dour, silent brother finally stood in front of her.

'Nothing's happened there, everything is just as it was before,' said Väino.

A bright smile appeared on Milvi's face, freed from worry. Väino contorted his face into a laughing expression, which didn't suit his sullen eyes at all.

'But you keep worrying,' said Väino. 'Don't be concerned about the weather because it doesn't pay. Whatever comes, comes anyway.'

Väino took a rucksack and a medical kit from the boat and brought them to the tent. Involuntarily, his gaze drifted towards the well site of his childhood. There, Milvi's slightly flawed operations came into view, and Väino went to drink from the mug placed there.

'Very good water,' he said, 'but you don't know how to make a well. Where's the shovel?'

Milvi handed over the shovel and Väino studiously began to dig the well. It was just like it had been with Dad and Uncle Gunnar. Väino threw out the water that had become muddy from digging and began to earnestly fill the new well. Clear water trickled swiftly into the ground cavity. Milvi watched the emerging water, spellbound.

Väino covered the well with plastic to keep out debris and insects.

'Did Herman tell you?' asked Milvi. Her brother's arrival made her happy.

'No,' said Väino. 'I worked it out myself when I saw that Herman's boat was gone. Did you come to work?'

'Yes, I'm tinkering about a little,' Milvi apologised, as if she was used to apologising to strangers for being too engrossed in her work.

'Tinker away, I won't bother you.'

'No, no,' Milvi countered. 'I'm glad you came. I'll be back there later. I should offer you food, but I don't have any.'

She looked at her brother's laughing eyes.

Väino patted his belly heavily.

'Don't worry, my body is full of goodness. I can hold out until tomorrow.'

'Are you staying till tomorrow?' Milvi's eyes widened.

'What are you going to say to Maret?'

'I told Maret that a summer holidaymaker started giving birth somewhere in Seemu Islet. Maret grumbled about why Ene isn't going, why does the chief physician have to go himself, when the midwife was available. And anyway, what have these holidaymakers got to do with us, let them come in at the right time. I repeated that I would not dare give the boat to the girl. If I tell her to go, I should take her there myself. I'm in charge. Who else was going to tend to a stranger on summer vacation on a Saturday? Maret won't let me go to sea alone with Ene.'

Väino talked about his scheming without the slightest hint of humour. Milvi shook her head. Maret had a very jealous nature, although Väino probably didn't give her a reason for it. In the village, however, even talking cheerfully with a female stranger was considered a suspicious act of love, because what a wonder that a person should even talk like that. Maret was even jealous of Milvi.

'You haven't tried fishing?' asked Väino.

'I don't have any tackle with me,' Milvi replied.

'I'm going to cast out a little fishing line,' said Väino. 'I haven't even had time to go fishing this summer.'

'Then where does your time go?'

'Ah,' Väino clapped his hands. He picked out his fishing gear and waded to the other side of the wide bank, to the old fishing spot.

Milvi started drawing plants again. In the city, she could create an entire environment around herself through one tiny detail of nature. Gazing at a snow patch glistening in the sun on the roof of the house opposite, with the early spring indigo sky above it, Milvi could effortlessly summon radiant snowy open spaces with the scent of snow, emanating pure freshness. It could also be done through a symbol placed in a work of art. Form, colour, word, sound, material: they created a new whole in which Milvi could live. Of course, the presence of a stranger could be tolerated if the gauntlet of hatred was not thrown directly in her face. Milvi avoided hostile work. It helped that she could protect herself from suffering in her life.

The wind had become stronger, fluttering Milvi's paper about. She gathered her work together. The sun went down, clouds had appeared in the sky. There was a chill in the wind. Milvi thought sadly that she would not last long like this: the cold and hunger would soon drive her back to the shore.

She made a fire and put the kettle on. She started peeling potatoes. Väino was doubtless hungry already. He was used to plenty of food.

The wind whirled between the stones and drove the smoke here and there. The clouds moved sporadically, skilfully circling around the sun and gliding back and forth in front of it.

Väino had caught a pike and returned over the stony ground, the shrubs and the sedge grass in the shallow water intruded with the noise of his black rubber boots.

'Well, how's this for a fish!" he showed the catch to Milvi.

The fish was a big and strong creature, its beautiful scales glistened with moisture, its slender tail hung down as Väino lifted it to show Milvi.

'I've already boiled the water,' smiled Milvi.

Väino pulled a knife from its sheath and began gutting the fish on a wide faded plank brought up from the beach. The entrails flowed out of the fish in a dark red and whitish colour. Tiny, devoured fishes glistened in the pike's stomach.

Later, as Väino stretched out in the tent and Milvi rested her chin on her knees in front of it, looking up at the clouds moving in the sky, she suddenly asked: 'Väints, tell me, do you sometimes see ghosts?'

'I do.'

'What kind?'

'Small, pale, neckless, fat ones with big mouths, they suck in everything around them. They are both brazen and intimidating at the same time, and they're looking at me, but their eyes are blind or they can't see me, and I can tell that instead of thinking, they have something else going on. They won't run away, they just keep moving forward, somehow sticking to the ground, so it is impossible to scare them or sweep them away. And there are more and more of them. Honestly, they make me feel fucking hopeless. The disgusting thing is that they have the shape of a person but are not people.'

'Are you afraid when you see them?'

'No fear,' answered Väino. 'Only dreary tedium sets in, and there is not a shred of hope.'

Milvi sighed.

'Are you drinking these days?' she asked sadly.

Väino did not answer.

After a while, he inquired morosely: 'Have you got what you wanted?'

Milvi turned to the question.

'I have been constantly rethinking what I've wanted,' she said. 'You remember when we were in High School, I really liked Köler.[1] Nowadays, no one would dare to admit this about their youth. Now I understand that Köler's symbolism showed me the direction that his soul desired; but he himself was held so strongly by the forms and tastes of his time that what he was able to show outwardly was horribly tainted by his surroundings. Now I sometimes think that maybe those outward signs are the only ones that can speak at all to someone approaching from somewhere else, from another time or place. Searching for content is a game played with signs, but in reality signs are like ritual activities that no one really understands any more, the content of which has no significant meaning. I want to find signs from which the contents haven't been drained. I want to get out of this game.'

'I haven't been following these problems so closely,' Väino apologised woodenly.

Milvi felt embarrassed.

'Of course,' she said. 'I'm just explaining it. You asked about it.'

'I asked if you got what you wanted.'

Milvi was lost in thought.

'I guess I got what I wanted. But these are all outward-facing signs.'

'Then the content is not satisfactory?' asked Väino with some animosity.

'I don't know,' Milvi said and smiled slightly. 'The content doesn't allow itself to be captured. What about you?'

'My life is screwed up.'

Milvi looked at her brother in shock.

'But…' she began, flustered.

'You are also targeting external forms,' Väino said bitterly. 'You remember when we went to school, you to the art institute and I to university, two children in two cities, with Mum and Dad left at home with one and a half roubles and a bunch of turnips to their names. They ate those turnips until payday, and they were happy to continue helping us as much as they could. I don't have to worry about subsisting on a diet of turnips. Maret wouldn't agree to do that either, she cannot be forced to the level of an animal. I can put Moonika through at least three higher education institutions and pay the admission for each and every one. The problem is whether Moonika even bothers.'

Milvi guessed that her brother's coming to the islet was not just a little secret fishing trip, but a painful impulse.

'Did something happen to you?' she asked cautiously.

'Nothing,' Väino said. 'Nothing has happened and never will happen, don't worry. Everything will go on as before, I do not matter any more. End of story. Tell me how Mart and Madis are doing, there hasn't been time to ask, you're always yapping.'

'They are doing well,' Milvi said without really thinking about her sons. 'Mart is going to get married, so it seems. Madis is working hard.'

'Hmmm,' said Väino. He didn't considers Milvi's sons for long.

The clouds had taken over the whole sky in the meantime. Without the sun, the isle took on a different appearance. The absorbing, fascinating peace of the island had disappeared. It looked old, worn, battered by the winds, it had endured everything and would continue that way.

Milvi would have liked to talk to her brother, somehow find a connection through words, but she couldn't; they hadn't had a chance to stay together as twins for a very long time, and so Milvi no longer knew her brother's inner voices. She knew that for years Väino's work has been overshadowed by the endless construction at the hospital, which Väino has to monitor as the chief physician. Mentioning the building works would hardly rouse her brother's senses.

'I saw that you have planted new roses,' said Milvi. 'You already have a lovely rose garden.'

'Do you know how much hope was been squandered by ploughing money into that house and garden?' said Väino, looking sharply at Milvi. He made a vague motion with his hand and turned his head away.

'Maret deals with the roses,' he continued wearily after a moment. 'You know, a cozy little house drowning in roses. Do you remember those ancient Roman orgies from history where the guests were buried under rose petals until they suffocated? I understand them now.'

Milvi was silent.

It was getting cold. It occurred to Milvi again that the cold and hunger would eventually drive them back to their houses.

She took a jacket from the tent and put it on.

'Let's go for a little stroll,' she suggested.

Väino rose with a grunt.

They went to the beach.

The sky hung like heavy dark cast iron, and the wind was blowing between the sky and the water.

'We'll get rain,' Väino said.

Her brother's gloominess was becoming overbearing for Milvi. The fact that this could happen to her brother also meant failure for Milvi.

They were twins.

They were given one life to live: Milvi had half of that life. Why didn't she keep in touch with her brother more often, since they had been born as twins, each with half the life of the other? But could she have done that? After all, her thirsty brother would still have rushed to the spring, where it was known that whoever drinks from that spring…

Heavy drops fell on their face and hands. A pattern showing the start of rain appeared on the rocks.

'Let's go quickly,' said Väino. 'It's going to start.'

They jogged through the beginning of the heavy rain. It was not until they were sitting in the tent that the downpour really hit. It was as if the roof of the tent protected them from a waterfall. The rain flowed noisily, thickening, and thinning in torrents. Milvi closed the tent opening.

They hadn't got wet, only the violent wind had buffeted them.

'It's pouring down,' said Väino, still panting from their hurried arrival.

Milvi took out a comb from her rucksack and started to untangle her hair in bunches, since it had become knotted in the wind.

The comb got wet in her hand. Somehow sticky wet, so Milvi looked inquisitively at the comb.

She was frightened and raised the comb higher before her eyes to look at it more closely. It was dark because of the rain, the clouds, and the closing of the tent. The comb looked bloody.

'Goodness, take a look, do I have a cut in my head?' Milvi said to Väino. 'The comb is wet with blood.'

Väino thoroughly examined Milvi's head. There was no wound.

'Then where did the blood come from?' Milvi said in shock, lifting the comb again.

Another droplet of blood appeared on the sturdy teeth of the comb, lengthening, gleaming in the darkness, until it had grown so large that it fell from the comb onto Milvi's lap.

The black comb dripped blood.

Anna

Aino Pervik

'Mum, give me a drink!' said Liisa.

Anna turned on a yellow night lamp and helped the girl slake her thirst. Liisa's lips were dark and chapped, her face was flushed and the heat of the child's body shuddered up Anna's arms through to the back of her head. The fever had risen further.

'Don't go,' Liisa pleaded in a hoarse voice. Anna put on a thick dressing gown and quietly carried the child to bed.

She didn't want to wake Mati, as her husband had to rise early in the morning, and lately he had been complaining of increasing tiredness. In the evenings, he sank into Anna's arms completely wiped out, and in the morning he required several mugs of doubly-strong coffee before he could do anything.

She would have liked to measure Liisa's fever, but the child had quietened down and Anna did not dare start messing about with a thermometer. Her darkly reddening daughter awakened a special tenderness in her, with a small dose of childhood nostalgia at its foundation. Her own mother had pampered Anna during illnesses, read to her and tried to satisfy all her wishes, as dark grey winter slush lay flattened outside the windows, Dad was still at work and Mum took time for Anna. It was nice to remember.

When Grandma lived with them, she didn't even come near Anna's bed during illness, she said she wasn't permitted to. Why did she say that, Anna thought in bewilderment now, an odd turn of phrase, rooted in some ancient way of thinking.

Anna remembered living with Grandma as a strange period. Grandma was in their home only for her last few years, that was after the death of her husband, which she could not get over. Served and tended to like some sort of unnamed burden. At the very end, she started to fear people, she kept asking if they had come to take her away already. Anna sometimes wanted to snuggle up to her, but Grandma did not want to touch the child and pushed her further away! Grandma refrained from touching people at all, as though she forbade herself contact with people, creating a boundary that should not be crossed. Not even a person's hand.

'Why did they have to give you this ugly name of mine,' she sometimes muttered when Anna leaned close to her. Anna remembered that. She could not understand at all why Grandma was talking like that, it was not the reason why the child was not given a cuddle, besides, there was nothing wrong with the name.

Grandma was Anna too. They even looked alike. In childhood, it was not apparent, at least not to Anna's eyes, but now that Anna was already approaching forty, she recalled her grandmother more and more often when she looked in the mirror. The similarity glowed from somewhere within, though their external features were quite different. This similarity surprised Anna all the more.

They already had something in common in life. This commonality was oppressive as a dark omen. Grandma had buried three men, Grandpa was the second. Anna's first husband Ruuben was also in the grave. Ruuben's death haunted her. No one could diagnose Ruuben's condition, he simply passed away as if for no reason at all. Just suddenly became very tired. It was terribly unjust, Anna was used to everything having an explanation and a reason. The confusion took its toll.

The doctors just shrugged and had nothing to say. Ruuben's mother hurled vicious, furious explanations all over the place: she blamed Anna for her son's death and despised her daughter-in-law with an intense, deep hatred. Her mother-in-law said that Anna had sucked the life out of Ruuben. Anna did not feel guilty about it. Ruuben was anxious to provide luxury at home, but that's why he worked himself so hard. Affluence sought Ruuben more than Ruuben sought affluence. After all, there was perhaps some truth in Anna's relatives' thinly veiled burning jealousy: that her husband's family really know how to make money.

Ruuben was very passionate towards Anna, and she lit the flame in him perhaps more greedily than necessary, but even so, passion does not bring about death. Her mother-in-law probably could not stand the lack of an explanation, and it was easier for her if she could connect the cause with her outsider daughter-in-law, especially since she never acknowledged Anna as her own: Anna and Ruuben had no children.

Mati turned on his side while sleeping, and his back emerged from under the covers. Anna went to adjust the duvet and pressed her cheek against her husband's warm, strong back. She was startled when Mati suddenly began gasping in his sleep, it was so scary that Anna shook him. Mati opened his eyes.

'You had a bad dream,' Anna said, horrified, 'you made such a horrible noise.'

'Yes,' Mati said in a weak plaintive voice, still confused by sleep. 'I dreamt that I was a horse, and a nightmare followed. Did I frighten you?'

'Of course you did!' said Anna. 'What a dream!' She was upset that her touch had summoned a nightmare into Mati's dreams.

'How is Liisa?' Mati asked.

'Hot,' Anna replied. 'Try to get back to sleep, I'll sit with Liisa. Does the light bother you?'

'It's OK,' said Mati, turning towards the wall.

Liisa had woken up to the conversation and now demanded in a serious adult voice:

'I need to pee!'

Anna helped the child to the potty.

The girl was even hotter than before, and when she was back in bed, Anna put a thermometer in her bottom.

A dark fear tightened in her throat. Once you have witnessed someone's gradual passing away, you cannot rid yourself of the experience. She knows death, and walks on the edge of the abyss at all times, and for her, all possibilities are open.

Her mother-in-law tried to keep Anna away from Ruuben's deathbed. She slandered her daughter-in-law with a lie and even hissed when Anna came. But Ruuben missed Anna and needed her to be near. It was hard for him to witness his mother's hatred, since Ruuben's mother was no longer able to control herself in front of Ruuben. On the last day, when Ruuben was visibly fading away, his head in Anna's hands, the mother-in-law had a fit of hysteria, she began to scream intermittently in Yiddish. Old Levinson, who was treating Ruuben, looked at both women in astonishment and began to calm Ruuben's mother by patting her on the shoulder, finally guiding her out of the ward and giving her something to take. A painful shadow slipped over Ruuben's face as he listened to his mother's pleas. Ruuben did not know much Yiddish, and when Anna asked what his mother had said, he replied that he did not understand.

He asked Anna to kiss him, and during that kiss he must have died. Anna could not precisely pinpoint the moment of death, she had never witnessed death. Yet after the kiss, Ruuben's life was gone, and after some time spent in fear, Anna called the nurse to look at him, who said that Ruuben had died.

Anna took the thermometer from Liisa. The column of mercury had risen strangely high and was now above forty. Anna gave Liisa an aspirin and went into the living room to get a bottle of vodka from the drinks cabinet. Her child should be rubbed with vodka.

Liisa shivered as Anna pushed the blanket off her and her nightie bunched up around her throat. Her tiny body was even skinnier when she was ill, and it was hard for Anna to look at her. When the cold cotton ball soaked in vodka touched Liisa, the child began to cry.

'Don't, Mummy,' she complained.

'Quickly, quickly!' Anna reassured the girl and she ran her hand swiftly over Liisa's body. 'Let's put the blanket back on right away!'

After the vodka rubbing, the child seemed to be getting better. She quietened down again. Anna looked at her. Her daughter's face was comically like Mati's. At this similarity, Anna sensed a pleasant shudder, she felt Mati's strength from it, and this strength, as it flowed into Anna through the resemblance, intoxicated her and lifted her up to a calm, happy surface. However, the darkness beneath the top layers did not disappear, the surface state seemed temporary and very much connected to Mati and Liisa.

The child's breathing became more regular and deeper. Anna started to calm down. She was gripped by unrelenting fatigue. The hours spent watching with worry through the night were exhausting, she wanted to go to bed. Anna was not willing, however, to leave the child unattended as yet, deciding to sit up for a while, and when the fever has definitely subsided, she can finally lie beside Mati and sleep.

Anna rested her head against the end of Liisa's bed. Her eyes started to close, the surroundings became blurry.

That strange memory came again, of an event that Anna had not experienced before, but it was an unusually clear and vivid remembrance. She must have seen it in a film or read it somewhere in a book that she later forgot but was heavily invested in at the time, so it started to return as a memory. Maybe she saw it in a dream. Anna had a disturbingly lively imagination. At night, this memory was real anyway, it could not be resisted. The recollection had tormented Anna even as a girl.

She remembered the reddish light of midsummer sunset, between the home on the hillside and the dark edge of the valley. Anna was a city kid, but in her memory her home was in the countryside. The slope was golden from the sun's radiance, and before the forest a shadowed area filled with a rising evening mist. The sun was setting behind the forest. The home at the top of the hill was full of gentle, peaceful evening light.

Along this hillside, down from the house towards the forest, she, Anna, was running, wearing white clothes; her heart pounding, the taste of blood in her throat. The fear she experienced as she ran there made her heart race even now.

Anna was chased by a large mob. She ran for her life, not pursued by strangers, but by her very own. Why, Anna did not remember. Equally, she did not know if she escaped them. What could have been wrong with her, to make her an outcast and chased by her own kind?

Anna forced herself to be more alert to escape the feeling of dread. The fatigue was intense. Liisa had been ill for several days and nights. At first, she vomited a lot, cried and was moody. In addition to the child's illness, Anna also had to complete a work deadline, and it was good that she could do it at home. Her strength was running low.

At least on this night, Liisa's fever had subsided and Anna

could rest. She carefully touched her daughter. Her head and hands were cool.

Liisa woke at the touch.

'Sleep, sleep,' whispered Anna. 'Mummy's going to bed too.'

Liisa smiled sleepily and stretched out her hands to Anna: 'Kiss!' she demanded.

Anna sat beside her child on the edge of the bed and bent down to kiss her. The girl grabbed her neck tightly with her hands, she was so cute and small wrapped in that soft blanket. Anna felt a life-giving freshness flowing from the child's body. The fatigue disappeared. Anna became alert, receptive. She noticed that the child's arms around her neck were weakening, slipping down her shoulders, falling heavily on the blanket. Anna wondered what had happened to Liisa.

Then, suddenly, there was a lightning flash of recognition of a repeated moment, a recurring event. She leapt up like a spring, took the poor child in her arms and lay her onto the bed next to Mati. Mati opened his eyes in shock and sat bolt upright.

'Take Liisa!' screamed Anna. 'I'm not allowed to touch her!'

Mati took the child into his arms.

'What are you yelling at!' he said angrily. 'You are scaring the girl.'

He slowly began to caress the whimpering Liisa.

'Come now,' he said to the child. 'Liisa's in Daddy's arms. Go to beddy-bye.'

The girl calmed down and made herself comfortable in her father's embrace. Her eyes closed.

'You're getting really confused, aren't you?' Mati rebuked Anna. 'Calm down, everything is fine. You see, nothing is wrong with Liisa any more. You'd better go to sleep, I'll put Liisa to bed.'

Anna's hands were trembling as she rearranged Liisa's bed. Mati lifted the child back into bed. Liisa turned herself on her side and bent her knees, as she usually slept.

'Now come under the covers,' called Mati, already in bed.

Anna hesitantly crawled beside him. A nervous jolt still flowed through her. Slivers of memories, fragments of sentences, all kinds of long forgotten observations, which had no sort of meaning before, but now in the close darkness of the night, acquired a terrible significance, and arranged themselves in a startlingly coherent relationship. It was something that in the cold light of day would seem like utter nonsense, but now it filled her with a stiffening fear. Anna started to feel sick.

She did not dare to look for support from Mati's warm body, although she knew that by clinging to him, she could instantly share in his peace.

She is not allowed, she really is not allowed.

Anna began to eagerly wait for daylight. She still did not know how she would fit this nocturnal awakening into her world, but the light of day would probably give her a clear mind and all her fear would disappear. After all, you cannot let ghosts mess up your life. Yet she shuddered in cold fear of herself. It was hard for her to resist the temptation to cling to Mati, to wrap her arms greedily around his shoulders and begin to absorb his bold, carefree vitality.

The Bench

Piret Raud

'Come, sit amongst us!' cried the one furthest on the right, and probably the youngest. She beckoned invitingly. I smiled vaguely and tried to pretend I couldn't see them, though actually, of course, I had seen them. They huddled on a long bench, like laundry left to dry on a line: each one old and decrepit alike, separate from the rest of the party area, yet all with their faces turned towards the Midsummer bonfire, their eyes fixed on the few dancers. Now, though, they were studying me.

In a panic, I searched for a polite reason to refuse, but nothing suitable came to mind. Madis had gone for the drinks and disappeared, and I did not notice a single acquaintance to latch myself onto. I didn't really know anyone here.

Then the one who sat to the left of the rightmost woman said: 'Come, come! Don't be proud!'

The woman's words left me with no other choice—I certainly did not want to seem arrogant. I went and sat in an empty spot next to the one furthest on the right.

'Madam is the new lady of the house at Metsa Farm, I suppose?' a voice now asked, which sounded distant, almost at the other end of the bench. She had wrapped herself in woollen shawls despite the warm evening, so that all that could be seen of her was a crinkled face with a sharp nose and thin lips.

'Yes, Lola is my name.'

'Milli,' the woolly bundle nodded with dignity. 'Milli Sepp.' She adjusted her plaid and gently nudged the granny sitting next to me, of whom I could only see a hazy profile.

'She is Vaike,' Milli said. 'Though Vaike doesn't talk much.'

So it was: Vaike did not react in any way, but looked straight ahead, faintly melting into the twilight. She was more like a spirit than a human being. Like a shadow with no forms, a grey uniform surface, with unclear outlines. A vague silent darkness.

It is possible that she hadn't heard what Milli had said earlier at all, more likely though, she simply didn't care.

'Maie,' the remaining woman, and next along from Milli, introduced herself, wearing a gorgeous silk dress with a wide collar. Her hair was bouffant and rigid, as if set by a hairdresser. Maybe she had been to the hairdresser in the village.

'Mare,' said Maie's neighbour, whose hair looked like she'd been dragged through a hedge backwards. 'I'm from the city too, but there is no need to be ashamed of it. We all know each other here.'

Next to Mare sat Riina, and Terje was beside Riina, and next to Terje was Kaire. Lilian and Eve were somewhere in there too. The bench was long, and I couldn't remember the names of all of them. The one I sat next to, and who had spoken to me first, introduced herself as Liis. She couldn't have been much older than me, perhaps just a little over thirty, but it seemed as though she were the same age as the others, as if the long bench had stretched Liis' years to an equal footing with the others.

'Metsa Farm has a good variety of blackcurrant,' said Riina, who was distinguished from the others by an uncommonly low voice that gave more weight to her words. 'The former lady of the house still made jam. She cooked up a hundred jars every summer, so it could be taken for a fever in winter. If you should be short of jars, I can give some to you. I have accumulated them over time.'

'Thank you,' I said. I didn't really have any plans to make jam, but I kept that to myself.

'You can get jars from me too,' Milli promised, and all the other women confirmed the same.

I thanked them.

The bench on which we sat was crude and strong, with a smoothly worn seat section and plenty of legs. The legs were coarse and sunk deep into the ground, as if the bench had stood there for centuries, until finally becoming one with the landscape. The women's legs looked as heavy as the bench's: some hidden in beige tights, though mostly bare, the straps of their open shoes carving grooves into their wide feet. These were feet swollen from standing, the feet of good working women, the kind that gently carry the gloom of all the world's troubles. Tirelessly and with a sense of duty, self-sacrificing. For now, though, they are resting, because sometimes they can. Still, it was a holy Midsummer night, a celebration of light.

'And rats. You probably have rats there too?' inquired Terje.

'Yes, there probably are some,' I admitted, blushing. 'They scratch at night.'

'That's what they do,' Terje nodded, and all the women on the bench hummed in agreement.

The mood sank. Now it was certain that they were indeed rats. Not mice, who seemed less powerful and more or less feasible to overcome, but actual rats. Big, with matted fur, bare tails dragging along the ground, and diseases in the corners of their teeth. Well, I'd guessed this before: I heard crunching and rumbling from inside the wall of the bedroom at night, and found droppings in the drawers of an old dresser moved into the pantry. The kitchen cabinets were otherwise scrubbed clean by the former owners, they betrayed nothing. But the racket was disturbing and frightening. And the scrabbling. It evoked the story of how during the war rats had devoured a slumbering person. They came out of hunger, after which all that was left were the remains chewed bare to the bones. Another time I left the lamp on at night, to give me the courage to go to sleep. The scrabbling did not bother Madis, he always sleeps an enviably deep sleep, especially here in the country, where the fresh air sweeps you off your feet.

'You don't have a cat?' Riina asked.

'No.'

'I can also give you a cat. I have accumulated cats over time.'

'You can also get cats from me,' Milli said, and the same was asserted by all the other women.

I looked for Madis; the news about the rats had to be shared. But he was nowhere to be seen.

'Your man has left you alone in the middle of the party?' asked the same woman who had thought I was aloof at first.

Krista was her name, I guess. Her eyes were red, a bit like a roach, but I couldn't tell if it was from crying or for some other reason.

'He went to fetch drinks,' I mumbled apologetically.

'That's what they do,' Krista nodded; it seemed to me that it was done with a little *schadenfreude*, and the women on the bench hummed in agreement. 'They like to drink.'

I wasn't going to argue with them, I wasn't going to say that, in actual fact, Madis rarely takes a beer or a glass of wine. I didn't want to upset them. They probably have different experiences with their men.

'Is he rough towards you otherwise?' inquired Mare.

'In what sense?' I didn't know what to say.

'Beating?'

'Beating? What?'

'You!'

'No. There's no beating.'

'Well, he'll get there,' Krista declared, with a glow of roach eyes. 'If he's not beating you now, he will definitely start soon.'

'If he beats you, then there's nothing to do but endure it!' added Milli gently. 'You will endure it! And think about what you can do to make sure a man has a better time at home.'

Again, the bench full of women hummed in agreement.

'If he strikes very hard and it hurts, then apply something cold!' said Riina. 'Ice, for example. You can get it from me, I have it.'

Ice was kindly promised by the others too. Only Vaike the Ghost was silent, as was Liis, who was sitting next to me, looking worriedly at her knees. It was now that I noticed the blue marks on her legs.

In the meantime, more dancers had appeared on the party floor—as is usually the case when twilight advances.

In the distance I finally caught sight of Madis too, who seemed to be looking for me. I waved to him, but he did not notice me, and I stood up so he could see me. At that moment, the bottom of my dress tore, having caught on the edge of the bench. To tell you the truth, I was sorry, it was my favourite dress—with a green butterfly pattern. While I was examining the torn spot, Madis disappeared again. But at least I now knew which direction to find him.

'I suppose I'm going to go,' I told them. 'It was really nice to meet you.'

'You're bored with us?' asked Kaire. Belligerently, to my mind.

'No, not at all.'

'Stay a little longer then!' Liis pleaded. There was a kind of tense fear in her voice, as if my presence was of vital importance to her. I understood her: besides Liis, I would have preferred different company to those sitting next to her. I preferred after all, to be on my way to Madis, to forget my worries, to laugh and to dance.

I didn't say anything. I was hoping that Liis' plea would slip away and dissolve, mixing with the rest of the vagueness beyond, but it did not happen. Something tense lingered in the air between us, waiting to decide on which side to fall: either selfishly indifferent or obligingly understanding. Either go and forget about this weird bench or stay for a while, get to know them, delve into their experience, be respectful, care. The bench full of women looked at me expectantly, condemnation hiding among handkerchiefs stuffed into their sleeves. They had thought of me as their own kind, believed in me, and at the same time I was failing them.

I fell back to take my seat. Not so much out of compassion for Liis as out of fear of Kaire's insight, because in fact I was bored with them. Or more accurately, uncomfortable. They were so different from me. But I didn't want them to realise that I thought so. I am not stuck-up. It isn't right to be superior.

'So, when are you expecting a little family?' asked the woman whose name had slipped my mind.

'Tomorrow's bus isn't coming just yet,' I tried cheerfully. 'But perhaps there is still time for that urgent matter.'

'Or maybe not?' said the woman whose name I had forgotten, suddenly becoming annoyed.

'At first it may seem like there's time, but it's too late afterwards.'

'Too late,' the other women's hum echoed in agreement.

'Of course, I've been thinking about it,' I said quickly. 'A child would be nice.'

'One child is definitely too few,' the other woman pronounced, whose name I had forgotten.

'Two is also insufficient,' added a nameless third.

'Also, three. Insufficient.'

Hum.

'Four is too many.'

Hum.

I don't know how much time may have passed before I saw Madis again, because time here behaved differently: it was both stationary in the moment and moving at an unusual speed. In turn, the minutes were folded, then pulled apart as a fan, and it was hard to tell when exactly one or another took place. Only this was certain: Madis was not alone, but with a strange young girl. They headed to the dancefloor. It wasn't a good feeling for me to watch them dance. The girl was beautiful. Natural somehow. She tossed her loose hair once to the right, once to the left. Not during slow dances, of course. Then her hair rested on her back, with Madis' hand on top.

All the women on the bench saw how they were.

'That's what they do,' Krista stated with a unanimous hum of agreement, and as I looked up at her, she winked at me with one of her roach eyes. 'They like young girls.'

Some part of me wanted to contradict them, to explain that they misunderstood the matter. That young woman out there is probably a relative, one of Madis' many cousins. It is also possible that she is the girlfriend of some coworker, a fleeting acquaintance, someone with whom Madis has no real association. Madis is just dancing with her out of politeness. Or just to pass the time because I have left him on his own.

Yet I didn't say anything because I lacked the courage to contradict them.

'This kind of thing has to be forgiven a man,' Milli said gently. 'They can't do otherwise, they simply need to sow their seed everywhere. It's an inner compulsion, bestowed by nature.'

'It is important to continue living,' said the woman whose name escaped me.

My eyes welled up.

'If you become sad, take valerian!' suggested Riina. 'You can get it from me, I have it. There are drops, and there are tablets too.'

They were all ready to share valerian with me. In the form of drops and tablets. They were all willing to help me, give advice, always be there for me. You can always count on them, they will not betray, they will have a clear direction and frequency, pressure and density. Happiness is in the little things, those who suffer live long, better to have half an egg than an empty shell. The kindness that had been eroded by years of experience moved closer and closer, the wisdom that had survived the winds of centuries came steadily along the edge of the bench and back again undaunted: they knew what was right, what was wrong, they knew how and for what. It was high time for me to get out of there.

'Thank you!' I said assiduously. 'Thank you! Thank you! Thank you very much! Really, thank you! Well, what would I do without you! Many thanks!'

I pressed my heels down decisively to get up.

They watched me with interest. They already knew I could not stand. They knew my dress was stuck on the bench. And not just a dress, but my whole bottom. It had sunk into the hollow of the bench, and following the shape of my body, was held in place by a strong grip.

I tried to get my legs in a better position so I could get

back up. Where the bench leg stuck to my calf a piece of flesh was torn right off where my tattoo was. I screamed because it hurt. Blood immediately began to seep from the wound, and a moment later it was oozing down my leg and dripping into the grass.

'You have to put a broad plantain leaf on top of the wound,' Riina hummed. 'You can get it from me, I have plenty of them growing in my garden.'

I tried to rock the bench, but it didn't move. I summoned up all my strength, but no—the weight of the women held it firmly in place.

'I can give you a plantain leaf too,' Milli hummed, and the other women thrummed the same. In an ominous tone, reminiscent of the sound emitted from old power lines on damp evenings. Inconspicuously, the hum had become incessant, quieter then louder, flowing and undulating, drowning out all other sounds, including the music from the dancefloor.

I tried to get up again, but to no avail. The only thing I achieved was that my buttocks were now bleeding too.

I called for Madis, but he didn't hear me. Understandably, because my voice was drowned by the drone of the bench.

I tried to scream over the hum, I shouted loudly and repeatedly, shrieking my voice hoarse, but he still didn't notice anything, and kept on dancing. I didn't give up and I didn't shut up: I was yelling like crazy, like a madman on a rampage, I was screaming even when there was no one left to call, when Madis and the girl had finished dancing and left, and I was silent only when Liis next to me put her hand on mine and squeezed it carefully. Soothingly. Compassionately and reassuringly. Liis' hand was dry and veiny, the skin around her fingers was shrivelled like crinkled paper. I did not dare look at my own hand.

Now Milli picked up the song. The song grew out of that very humming: she began quietly, with a trembling voice and fragmented lyrics, and then it swelled powerfully and became less humming and more song-like. She was soon joined by Maie and Mare, then several more women, and before long the whole bench sang, except for Vaike, of course. When the song had reached Liis, I suddenly opened my mouth as well. I don't remember ever learning those songs, yet I knew all the words, not just the choruses, but the melodies flowed naturally from within me, as if they were my own songs. The songs dragged on and were full of repetition, going back to the beginning again and again, getting nowhere and without end. There was something soothing and invigorating about this monotony, it sounded like a mantra that helps keep the mind together and in the right direction. Something that doesn't let an intruder or a stranger get in the way, or shake your peace of mind. The other revellers paid no attention to us; too busy dancing. Maybe they did not want to hear us at all, preferring a different beat. A rhythm that was familiar to me, that used to feel so homely, which slipped further away from me with every verse.

The song ended the same way as it had begun: the bright voices of the women became more and more monotonous, until they retreated into the dullness of the old powerlines to fade into silence. Now I noticed that Vaike wasn't there any more. Where the granny had previously sat, a grey emptiness yawned. As though she had completely merged with the twilight. I guess that's the way it is. At first, there is a desire to change things, a yearning to speak out, then the boundaries disappear, and then that's it.

Maie said something, and Mare too, they talked, along with the other women. Millie was the only one who did not speak. I didn't really follow what they were saying. I just nodded in agreement. My former anxiety had left me, and there was no sadness. It was just like that.

At some point, the sun was setting, and the sky was slowly darkening. Yet the bonfire was bright enough to illuminate the surroundings, and I could see that the bleeding from my biggest wound had stopped. I stayed still and quiet, nonetheless. There was no desire to scratch, not even to scare away the mosquitoes. Maie, second from the end of the bench, wrapped herself in a shawl.

Madis was still nowhere to be found, and I was not expecting him much any more, but when I spotted the girl who was dancing with Madis coming towards us, I was roused from my lethargy. Suddenly, the hope sprung in me that Madis has sent her to help me, or that she has a message from Madis for me. A good message, of course, for example, that Madis is about to arrive, only a little longer now. However, as the girl got closer, reached us and came to a stop without engaging us, I realised that there was no meaning in it—the girl had come close to the bench by chance.

She stood there and looked at her phone, her head slightly skewed, her skirt barely reaching her knees. The legs that stretched out from under the hem of the dress were slender and long. Not tanned to brown—tanned skin is not in fashion among young people—but uniformly pale like a doll's. Smooth and uneaten by insects, light and carefree. Alive. Just made for dancing.

I had no anger towards her. Quite the opposite. I liked her.

Liis nudged me, but even I knew what I had to do.

'Hey!' I shouted. She lifted her gaze from her phone and saw us. 'Come sit amongst us!'

The girl hesitated.

"Come, come! Don't be proud!" cried Liis.

The Paper Bird

Piret Raud

I had always known that I was in danger of turning into the kind of woman who in old age walks the city streets and yells angrily to herself and bangs her handbag against lampposts to try to find a way of escaping the anxiety that has accumulated inside her. Now that moment had come.

'Shit!' I yelled and swung the bag around until bang! I felt the compact crack inside it. When Allan was still alive, the simple breaking of household crockery helped. A little bit of crying, then throwing a tasteless gifted bowl or old plates scratched by forks and already in need of replacement, breaking to pieces on the kitchen floor—it always brought relief. There was something dignified and aristocratic in breaking dishes, the shards on the kitchen floor were a firm statement that emotions are more important than reputation—that a person is more important than anything else. But after Allan's death it did not help any more. There was no longer Allan, who would have helped pick up the pieces later, there was no longer his gaze, in which horror mixed with admiration for my passionate nature that shone so brightly. There was no Allan, he hadn't been there for a long time, just like there wasn't a kitchen floor attacked by broken dishes.

In my new apartment, I felt like a melon slice encased in plastic wrap. I know that Ivika wanted the best for me—my daughter always only wanted the best for everyone—and the fact that the building had just been completed meant an enormous improvement in her eyes. An apartment in a brand new building was a sensible capital investment in every way, an asset that will make her happy even after my death. But I, who had to live there, missed the high ceilings and the windows through which the wind would blow, and the creaking parquet underfoot, whose panels lifted off the floor with cheerful ease. It is true that the new home also had parquet but made as if from a single glassy piece that shone like a piano top. In the first few days, I did not really dare to step on it, because who wants to walk on a piano? In an extreme case, perhaps some self-absorbed slutty singer who has no respect for the dignified instrument. And so I would glide over it, rather than walk. The awkward alienation disappeared after only a few days, when a layer of dust had formed on the floor (it turned out that dust also lives in this sterile place) and I did not hurry to wipe it off.

However, more than anything else, I missed the light of my former home—the ray of sunlight that slid obliquely across the entire living room, making the glass vase placed on the dining table shine like a ball of fire, and in the spring months the tulips inside the vase too, as well as a portrait from my youth, which was hung on the wall above the vase—how beautiful I once was! No, it certainly wasn't dark in the new place, but the sun shines through the windows on the first floor in a different way than the fifth floor, where the sky is closer. 'The first floor is good,' Ivika said over and over when we talked on the phone. 'It's best for an elderly person.'

That was Ivika's opinion, I wasn't so sure about it myself.

Was I even sure of anything?

Maybe it all started with washing the windows. Incidentally, washing windows in the old home was no laughing matter, it was a big undertaking. Not because it was on the fifth floor, but because of the windows themselves. The windows there were old and double-glazed, the frames clumsily held together by screws. Since the position of the window frames had sunk down, it was quite a task to unbolt the screws, especially since during the last renovation the painter had sloppily covered them with thick paint. Once, Allan would have helped me, but now I had to do it myself. I scraped the paint off the screws with a butter knife and used an old clunky screwdriver to turn with all my might, which made my palms tender. After finally prying the frames open, I noticed that the inner glass did not need a special clean, and I immediately started working on the outer part.

It was a windier day than average—the first day of spring—and the fresh air pouring in from outside filled me with strength and vigour. A desire to become cleaner and better together with the windows, to start a new chapter in life that would make me different (and happier!) for all the coming years, which was stronger than the faint hopefulness that I had felt a few months earlier while admiring the beautiful New Year's fireworks from the same window. In retrospect, it could be said that it was a life-changing moment in a way, when a piece torn from a roll of paper towel suddenly fell from my hand and leisurely floated down. I watched with interest how the current of air carried the paper here and there at will and how it performed a strange pirouette like a figure skater on ice before finally falling on the asphalt in front of the building.

The sight was so captivating that I tore another strip off the roll and let it fall on purpose. How much more beautiful it would be if coloured paper floated in the air, I thought, and brought a pack of napkins with a vibrant flower pattern from the chest of drawers, which I threw out of the window one by one right there.

The next day I found a book in the supermarket that provided instructions on how to fold all kinds of things out of paper, and as I was flipping through it, I noticed a picture of a bird that looked a bit like an airplane, and the author of the book promised that if it was folded from a large, lightweight sheet of paper, it would fly. I bought the book without hesitation as well as a roll of wrapping paper.

At home, I immediately started crafting. The paper I'd bought was thin, yet strong and pleasantly matte under the fingers, not slippery. The pattern was lovely: golden bunches of berries looked beautiful against a red background. For the bird, a properly squared sheet was needed, which was not so easy to cut, because the paper tended to curl up. Overall, making the bird turned out to be more difficult than I had thought, although this complexity was not unpleasant, but rather interesting. I used my fingernail to sharpen the folds, turned the bird one way and another, trying to understand the logic of the folding, and when I noticed that I had gone wrong, I took it apart again to get it back on track. I did not even notice how time flew by: all my attention was alternately on the paper and the book illustrations, it wasn't the kind of lack of awareness towards one's surroundings that ends in fatigue and disappointment, but the most pleasant kind of preoccupation, which culminated in the triumph of completing a task. Ivika had advised me to find a hobby to keep my mind off 'all kinds of bad things,' as she put it. Folding suited me well. Folding was unexpectedly uplifting.

At the same time, I was instantly reminded of that poor sick Hiroshima girl, a victim of exposure to atomic bomb radiation, who had folded nearly a thousand origami cranes in order to survive and get well—that is what the old Japanese belief promised, which in reality, of course, didn't help the poor girl. And I began to feel ashamed that my bird, put together so clumsily, had no nobler purpose than to amuse a bored old person. Yet we all live our own lives, and it wasn't my fault that the poor child's hometown was so brutally bombed in her time. Besides, even an old woman like me can have her own hopes and aspirations in life, and this slightly creased little bird was perfect for the fulfilment of my personal dreams.

In any event, I finished my bird, and it looked almost exactly like the one that was printed in the book. At first, I tried to fly the bird in the room, but there was not enough space, and besides, I had not made it as a house bird. My bird's flight arc had to be many times higher than some caged parrots. I opened the freshly washed window and threw the bird with as much velocity as I could towards the linden trees growing outside. Incredibly, my carefully crafted handiwork really flew and even its wings flapped in the wind just like a real bird, and it was indeed a wonderous sight. Fortunately, it did not get caught in the branches of the trees or get stuck anywhere—it was quite thoughtless of me not to think about this possibility earlier—but fell beside a tree where a man was standing. The man picked up the bird from the ground and waved at me.

'Ahoy, madam! Did you throw this?' he called.

'Yes,' I shouted back. 'Wait! I'll be right there!'

On any other day, I would not have been particularly excited about the possibility of dealing with a stranger, but that afternoon was different—it was exhilarating. I flew down the stairs like that paper bird, ruffling my hair on the way to make it look fluffier. Only when I was leaving the door of the building did I force myself to walk with a dignity commensurate with my age.

The man proved to be a scrawny old chap a little younger than me, as you can often find lounging on a bench next to a liquor store in the summer, so my initial excitement was greatly cooled. Still, I started laughing when he introduced himself.

'Romeo,' he said, bowing slightly, and handed me the bird with dignified solemnity.

I invited him to drink tea with me, and he started visiting.

Ivika did not like Romeo, even though he had been sober for several months and took full responsibility for his sobriety. And although he lived in one of the city's many social housing estates, and life there could not have been comfortable, he was never inclined to stay over with me and showed no sign of becoming the master of the house. That's probably what Ivika was afraid of. Ivika, who had not lived in her childhood home for decades, so I don't think she had any right to interfere in my life at all.

'You don't take him too seriously, Mum?' she asked me once, and it was downright shameless.

Of course I took Romeo seriously, and I took myself even more seriously than the man—my passion, my desire.

We met almost every day and mostly at my place, not outside the house—where especially would we have to go? We lay down on the sofa in the living room, and I let Romeo smoke there, even though Ivika had made some nasty comments about the smell of smoke that lingered all over him. (Allan never smoked indoors.) I do not remember that we talked much, and indeed I still don't know much about Romeo: what kind of boy he was during childhood, whether his family were Reds or those who kept their fists in their pockets and endured everything in silent repression; whether the reason he had started drinking was unrequited love, or had love become unrequited while he was already drinking; what was his favourite dessert, what kind of music did he like, whether he believed in God. It did not interest me. Something else was important to me. He was kind, he was very kind, he was a good man. That was enough.

We lay there very close together and watched the evening sun stream over the broken parquet, making the floor glow warmly, and then we sat on the windowsill, and I threw the paper bird and we admired how it flew through the air, flapping its wings—each time in a different way. And when the bird had landed, Romeo ran down the stairs to fetch it from outside and bring it to me so that I could throw it again. And when the bird got tired after many flights, we folded a new one. We made a lot of birds, and they were all different colours—I acquired blue, yellow, green and purple patterned wrapping paper—but always the same shape, and I have to say that Romeo's hands were just as adept at working on paper birds as he was on me. He was sweet, that Romeo of mine, and made my old heart beat faster, and his folded birds seemed alive and flew a good distance. He was a good man.

He was probably a good man on that other day too, but I was tired myself. I would rather have sent him back to the door when he arrived—friendly and kind as ever—but I didn't, I invited him in and made tea. As we sat down at the dining table, however, it seemed to me that Romeo was a little different than usual. The way he raised the cup to his mouth and then put it back on the saucer with a thud, and the speed with which his Adam's apple moved up and down his carefully shaven, skinny neck to the beat of his swallowing, expressed a determination I hadn't seen in him before, and it irritated me. I did not understand why anyone had to drink tea as if he were singlehandedly shooting an entire cavalry regiment with a machine gun. I would have liked Romeo to go away, to leave me alone, but I said nothing. I suffered in silence. Later, when we lay on the sofa, I did not have to regret my silence, because then he was back to his old self. 'Sweetheart,' he said as the sun coming through the window shone directly into my eyes, and it was meant to be.

Then we stepped onto the windowsill to fly the bird that Romeo had folded the night before. The bird in Romeo's hand was red, just like the very first bird I had made. The same red as Romeo's shirt, which was a little too big for him. A new shirt, which he had received as a donation from the church, and which did not smell of smoke, but of a stranger.

Romeo's hands holding the bird were slender and bony, fingers as thin as quills, and the skin around his wrists as tight and slim as the paper from which the bird was made.

'I'd like to try throwing,' Romeo said. 'You're always the one who flies them. Maybe you'll let me today?'

I did not like the sound of Romeo's voice. That determination again. It wasn't his business to demand anything. Such a good and kind man does not do that! I didn't answer him, but he asked again and I still did not answer. And then he asked more and more. And more. And his dry hands holding the bird moved once to the left and then to the right, as if they were floating a rubber duck in a bath.

I am absolutely certain, as sure as the police had been, that it was Romeo—a homeless man with an unfortunate fate—who finally threw the bird out of the window, and that it was he who jumped after the bird. Just as Allan had fallen from the same spot several years ago. He too. It couldn't have been me sitting on the windowsill next to Romeo, just as I had been close to Allan when he was washing those lovely old windows. It could not be me pushing Romeo to see if his skinny body in a giant red shirt could fly. Does he lightly flit towards the blue sky, do the air currents keep him aloft, do his shirt sleeves flutter in the wind like the wings of a paper bird? Did they flutter? I think so. What a flight!

I stood for a while next to the lamppost, the handle of my handbag tightly squeezed between my fingers. I stood as though I were another post of the same type. A blurry regret mixed with unintelligible thoughts—uninvited thoughts—pressed upon my shoulders, but I did not let them weigh me down. Instead, I opened my handbag and took out my compact. The case was damaged. The plastic clasp was broken and the mirror was cracked. A broken mirror—seven years of bad luck in love. I looked in the mirror and saw a familiar old face, many times more cracked than the mirror itself, and felt a momentary dizziness.

Please, please, for better or worse! But let it be inspiring, let it be touching, let it be beautiful! Let love be like the evening sun, which flows over the broken parquet and makes the floor flush with warmth, if only for a few minutes; let it be like a red paper bird that is carried by the wind, lifting me up again and again from the ground and sending me to the heights, creating the illusion of endless flight! May I still have something to look forward to!

While powdering my face, I noticed that a tiny shard had dropped out of the mirror and scratched my nose. It was just a little scratch and did not bother me at all. I gently put the broken compact back in my bag and started walking towards my new home. Come to think of it, it was actually quite cozy there.

When the Boys Came

Kätlin Kaldmaa

There had always been boys. In the sense that everything was fairly distributed so that if one household had four daughters, another was blessed with mostly sons, and their sisters were not taken into account. They were just regular girls. Girls were here. When two brothers once tried to stubbornly chop wood ('Take your hand off the chopping block, or the axe will hit it.' 'I won't take it away.' 'You will.' 'I won't.' 'You will.' 'I won't.' 'Get your hands off me.' 'I won't take it away.' 'Then I'll have to land the axe on the block.' 'Strike away if you want. I won't take it away.' 'You will.' 'I won't.' So, for a quarter of an hour, the villagers watched this wrangling and laughed) and the axe fell and the finger with it, though only they (and the girls) knew that it was because of girls. And there was that other time when another brother in a workshop picked up a 380-volt industrial wire in his bare hands, shuddered and convulsed, and the magic of electricity lifted him a metre above the ground and dropped him like a bundle of rags, well, that was also because of girls. The boys weren't even ten yet. The finger was sewn back on, and the electricity left a deep red mark on the boy's palm for life.

The boys were as ubiquitous as mosquitos and annoying as elk flies. There was no way around them. So, they were dealt with like ordinary annoying insects. They roamed (together with the girls) through the woods for days, searching for a bear's den and a thirteenth-century church, excavating the ruins of a manor house, and when grown-ups chased them away with pointless pretexts, they dug wherever they happened to be, and always found something archaeological, something worth investigating, a burnt school notebook from the war, where the writing had been lifted luminously from the black pages by the fire, so that the exceptionally neat handwriting of the schoolchildren of that time embarrassed the finders for a moment, which they soon got over, and these burnt schoolbooks were their greatest treasures, until they crumbled to dust despite their careful reading and study, or other gems like old-fashioned medicine bottles, bent by the fire where they should be straight, and straight where they should be curved, or a vase with a strangely broken edge, whose material has yet to be agreed upon.

The boys and girls were together day after day. Quickly, first thing, hurriedly and leisurely, head over heels, with everything completed that the parents who had gone to work had told the children to do, or it was postponed until the evening, which was riskier, because the parents could catch them out with their chores still in progress, and trouble and harsh words were waiting, and then you would be outside, out. Outside! 'Are you coming outside?' These words carried the complete infinity of the world that the boys and girls discovered in their daily roaming and playing, metre by metre, hectare by hectare, kilometre by kilometre, so that every day this space became bigger and wider and more exciting, with more people and things to do, and little cottages covered with charcoal tar paper, inhabited by wicked old people living in little houses in this world. Outside! Like that time when they decided to be sweet and good and worthy of Timur, who in books went around helping out the elderly, and chop the wood of that great auntie who lived far away, across the river, because she had no one to help her at all, and she moved so slowly that it took her all day to do her shopping, the boys and girls had seen it for themselves.[2] When that poor and quiet old person saw that her house was surrounded by boys who, despite being barely older than ten, were taller, bigger and undoubtedly more capable than her, she went out of her mind (outside!)—she rushed out of the house at unexpected speed, fumbling with a cane, a burning log in her hand grabbed from under the stove, she brandished and waved it as if possessed by an evil spirit, screamed and cursed like an old sailor, swearing at the children, to say that yet again someone—someone!—wanted to drive her out (outside!) of her very last abode, and that she would rather set fire to it with her own hands than let these kids take her house. The boys lost their nerve with all that cursing and cleared off, the girls close at their heels, and when they came to a stop upon reaching the river, the breathless girls said, 'Now let's go back and finish this thing. We'll go and talk to the auntie, and you'll stay back behind the wood shed until we let you come out.' The boys did not feel very confident, but girls are girls, and boys cannot oppose them. Quietly, they hung back, and silently the girls, well-behaved and polite, their pigtails in a tangle, their cheeks burning, went to Aunt Salme, who had no living relatives, although she had once had a large household with twenty cows and three farmhands, and back then her own boys and girls who had all been busily working for days and demanding food, and talking to her as only girls can talk, and soon the boys were cutting up logs and laying them in a row under the eaves to shorten the distance to carry them into the room, and the girls were clearing the living room and weeding the flower bed, so that midsummer phloxes and daisies were standing out from among the thistles, orache and ground elder that had grown half the height of the house. Thus, the window became whiter and the sun shone on the thick layer of salt sandwiched between the two window frames. The curtain, blackened from dust and fly droppings, after being washed and soaked in warm, soapy water, with the help of the children's feet, turned ivory like a bridal veil, and when the windows were washed, Aunt Salme did not want to leave the curtain hanging in the window any more, because who came here besides the wind and rain, and it looks better that way too. Outside.

Another thing that bound the boys and girls together on rainy summer days, when a grey wall towered above the window, was reading. Sometimes they took shelter in the cool rooms when the sun had lasted too long, when drought brought thunder and rainless bolts of lightning into the sky.

Books were read by the ton, and lines of writing equalling tens and hundreds of kilometres were devoured. Within a few years, the equator was circled. On reading *Romance of the Three Kingdoms*,[3] there were pieces of paper and later notebooks filled with family trees and lineages, which, when the more curious began to compile their own trees and lines of descent, they could ask their parents and living grandparents about them—'What are you talking about here, these aren't children's games, go and do your own thing, have the beets been hoed yet?'—and while reading *Genghis Khan*, the boys and girls talked about what horrors Genghis Khan's men did to the women and children of the places he conquered, the power that blazes in great men, things that neither boys nor girls were allowed to know of, and which were never mentioned, though all felt the anxiety of the unspeakable, and when one of them drew an illustration in his reading-book to depict what he had read, women with severed breasts dripping with blood and a warrior with the curved sword of the Khan, who piles the slaughtered children in a heap, in the autumn he was called to see the school's principal at once, and at home he received such a scolding from his parents, it was as if the curved sword had been in his hand and not in that of the warrior in the book.[4]

And no one understood when and how it happened that at eight years old these same boys and girls were still fighting, everyone with everybody else, with their little hands and feet and fists and nails, and at ten years old they were the ones who were scattered everywhere at all times, and without stopping would rush through the whole village and all the other villages like a whirlwind, and they were the ones who, with all their mixture of pre-teen greedy insatiability and childish all-encompassing innocence, gobbling up every last finger-sized baby cucumber in every person's greenhouse, then at the age of twelve, those same boys were fighting with all their hands and feet and fists and nails at school parties over the same girls, over who would go to the dance with them next, and the girls instead chose some other third or fourth boy for the sake of teasing, who they did not care for in the least, because they are independent after all and not for a moment to be disturbed by the shenanigans of these foolish boys.

It was not long after these fights, just a few years of growing up, when the boys started coming. Initially, they came with scooters, tractors, motorcycles, trucks, though not combine harvesters, which were not to be entrusted to the hands of youth, such machines, representing the wealth of responsibility, were driven by men of maturity and good sense. Later they came with Zhigulis, Moskvitches, Audis, Fords and BMWs. Zaporozhets was too feeble to come, and Mercedes beyond any possibility.

There were all kinds of boys. Boys came from near and far. The boys wrote letters—the postman was always delivering something to the girls' letterboxes—and they brought flowers, both plucked from the meadow on a summer's night, their trouser legs still damp, and long-stemmed roses straight from a garden, which in no way resembled the roses that grew under the girls' living room windows, the ones whose brightly coloured flowers always reached up to look through the windows at the end of summer. There was an awkwardness to how these flowers changed hands the first time, and the blatant superiority with which later flowers were received, their sisters were told to arrange them in a vase. Because they had to go now.

Yes, when the boys came, it was time to go. With their helmets on, the girls sat on the motorbikes behind the boys, and while they had to learn very quickly that you needed to hold on tightly to the boys on the motorbikes if you wanted to stay on the bike, it took some time before they learned to lean in the right direction when cornering, or rather, to set yourself free, so as not to work against the joy of movement and freedom. There was no stronger feeling than heading nowhere on the empty roads at night, with air, drops of water and snowflakes flying in your face, especially for those girls, the braver girls, who learned to drive themselves and with whom the boys had to learn that you must hold the driver tightly with both hands to stay in the saddle. For a long time, tightly grasping and speeding together wordlessly against the wind remained the greatest expression of intimacy. And sometimes, as an alternative to riding, sitting somewhere on the shore of a lake, some boys, the bolder boys, dared to put an arm around a girl's shoulders, and so they sat there, without saying much, until it was time to go again. Swimming together naked in the moonlight, however, was not achieved until a dozen years later. But anyway.

When the first girl had gone—and it had happened so imperceptibly, so casually, so naturally, and the boys who came, there weren't many of them, because she had narrowed down her choice pretty quickly—succession was now in the hands of the younger girls. A few years passed, almost devoid of boys and endless running around, years of growing up, the younger girls were five, six, seven years younger than the older one, and then suddenly it all happened at once, like a three-hurdle race, and those boys, who now began to hurtle along the grassy driveways in their vehicles, couldn't even count the girls. Turned into mud from the spinning wheels, the road had to be asphalted in the first summer.

The boys came. Rarely alone, more often in twos, threes, fours, fives, there was endless bragging and one-upmanship between them.

Mud flew from under the wheels, flowers were left with the mothers, the girls always flying, flying, flying, long loose hair was never braided when a ride was taken on a Jawa, so it caught all the rain, wind and snow, and there was no magic trick to getting things out of their hair, only the girls themselves, who combed and brushed each other's hair in their rooms, and while doing so kept giggling, squealing, laughing out loud, because the boys had used their magic power, had bound the girls to them, seemingly invisibly at first, but present in the grains of truth hidden in the gossip, which the girls never failed to notice.

Oh, what a sight it was! The twinkling lights in the early morning marshes, when the clothes were damp from being out all night, almost wet, but the hearts in their young breasts were beating so fast that the pulsating blood left no part of the body cold. A chorus of birds could be heard, as it turned from day to night, then suddenly died away, and around four o'clock it began again with the full force of life. From the high tower, one could see fires being lit in the surrounding villages, and in the lighthouses, it was as if all those fires were ignited on land and water at the same time. And in the winter, in Soviet times, on that day when it was not permitted to bring a spruce tree into a room and no candle could be lit, they still went to the cemeteries to light a flame at the graves of the dear departed, and those were the nights when, despite the cold temperatures, they drove, hair frozen solid, exceptionally slowly from one cemetery to another, to pluck from the distance the rays of light rising from the trees that illuminated this extraordinary one-night world made up of fractals where one could never, in any way, reach the end. There was no talking during those nights, which had been anticipated all year.

Then when the two-wheelers became four-wheelers and somehow all the boys and girls could no longer fit in one place, things started happening to the boys and girls who were paired off, things that were not spoken about to the others, yet became apparent. Among themselves things were no longer the same, bragging and gossiping were no longer the priority. The boys were now allowed inside the rooms. They praised the mothers' cooking and talked about sport with the fathers. And if one of them could memorise the winners of the Olympic Games, they got a higher seal of approval than the others. In the rooms, the boys and girls were as quiet as fleas. You could have gone to listen at the closed doors, but nothing much could be heard. If at all, a bit of conversation. A noise. And that stopped too.

And then, one morning, the day arrived where all the boys had come, and the house was empty of girls. Mum was sitting in her room, in an armchair meant for quiet reading, though not reading, just like that, with her hands in her lap, and a man who was not the girls' father, but who had long since come into the household where all these girls were, stood behind her, his hands firmly on her shoulders, and they were as quiet as the girls in their rooms, when the boys came.

Shitty Story

Kätlin Kaldmaa

You fill your pants before you get through the airport door.

There is almost no traffic early in the morning, so the taxi ride only takes three quarters of an hour, but already in the car you can feel it building up, building up, so you cross your fingers and hope you make it. You don't make it. There is a security guard on the door who wants to check all the boarding passes. Well, you don't have yours yet, so you already know what will happen. Basically, it all happens before you even get to the security guard. Quietly.

You sit on the toilet for a long time, hoping that everything's finally done, you throw away your underwear and line a new pair with toilet paper. It rustles a bit when you're walking, but that's no big deal.

Before getting on the plane, you sit on the throne five more times. At least it's real here, not a ditch by the road. This year's Independence Day speech by the Indian Prime Minister mainly comprises a list of how modern toilets have been built in several villages and how many hundreds of tons of faeces have been removed from the streets.

Before food is served on the plane, you go to the loo four times. Fortunately, the flight attendants do not have time to notice you, and it probably happens to half the people here. Your stomach is insanely empty. The food is truly magnificent, it even smells good. Emirates, they really know how to do it. You nibble on some rice. You can feel how it builds, how it builds, and you're already on the can again before the dishes are cleared away. Yes. It's. Good.

You have to go to the privy six times before you manage to get a little nap. So far so good.

You wake up, your stomach is terribly empty. Breakfast is coming! Scrambled eggs. Well, you can still eat scrambled eggs.

No, you can't. Before the plane starts to land, you manage to go to the toilet eight times and you would be happy to sit there for the entire descent. But that is not permitted.

You fill your pants before you get off the plane.

Before passport control, in the toilets you throw your underwear in the bin, take the next pair from your handbag and hope for the best.

There is a pharmacy on the other side. What luck!!! You buy two boxes of Imodium and wet wipes. You take three Imodium tablets. That should help a bit. Your stomach is really empty. You do not dare eat. You go to the lavatory a few more times before you take the city bus. So far so good.

You have a few days off before your next event. You go to the hotel, on the way you wheel your suitcase to the nearest underwear shop and buy three pairs. This should do.

The first day you sleep in the hotel, you don't notice much. At night, you wake up with an empty stomach. Well, you're groaning with pain when it's empty. Fortunately, this is Barcelona, your city, and you know where you can eat here at night. You buy a packet of biscuits, bananas and mineral water, there is no point in taking a risk.

You eat two bananas and five biscuits and wait. Nothing. You're still waiting. Nothing. You fall asleep instead. And when you run to the toilet half asleep, you first slam into a wall and only after that do you find the right door.

You fill your pants before you find the bathroom door.

Fourth day of diarrhoea. Lots of traffic between the bedroom and the bathroom, luckily you can wash your underwear while sitting on the toilet. It's not easy, even water seems to be solidifying in your guts. And then it turns liquid again.

The next day is the event. A discussion panel on stage. You don't dare eat anything, just in case, you dose up with four Imodium tablets. You cannot be too careful here. Outside, you dash from one bar to the next, so that if you have to run, you can sprint immediately. It goes well. You reach your desired location without incident.

Before the event, you sit on the toilet for ten minutes just in case. Nothing. So. It seems to be holding. You put powder and blush on your face to hide your grey complexion, and you go on stage. The conversation is fascinating and engaging, you pull yourself together to keep up with the southern gesticulations, and… ten minutes before the end of the conversation you rush off in a whirlwind.

You fill your pants before you reach the toilet. You throw away the underwear and line a new pair with tissue paper. You drink a little water. Your stomach is truly empty. You go to a cafe with the other panellists to continue the unfinished conversation, and drink tea. Green. Maybe it will stay in there a little longer. Others drink wine. The conversation is certainly fascinating, but you don't pay much attention, you wait for signs of the next outbreak.

The next day you fly to Berlin. The seminar and your boyfriend are waiting there. You take three Imodium tablets, don't eat anything, and don't drink anything. Well, it should stop now.

The flight goes well. You go to the bathroom, but only for prophylaxis purposes. Your boyfriend has come to meet you, but you do not have the strength to be overjoyed, and fall into a sleep-like state in the taxi.

This situation continues throughout the day, your boyfriend tries to be intimate a few times, you fight him away and crawl into the bathroom. At least you have the courage to drink now. The Imodium seems to be staying down.

On the eighth day of diarrhoea, the seminar begins. Fortunately, you don't have to give a long presentation, it's all about discussions and planning. You drink coffee, you are afraid that otherwise you won't get through it. By the second half of the day, you cannot resist eating a few biscuits.

After the seminar, dinner is in the restaurant. Four courses. You can't not go there, it is the most important networking session. And as already mentioned: f-o-u-r c-o-u-r-s-e-s.

You haven't eaten in two days. And everything that was eaten before has long gone. Your stomach is terribly empty.

First you locate the toilets—there are only two of them—and strategically position yourself in a sensible seat. The closest one, so you can run promptly when needed. Your stomach is really empty.

Everyone is drinking wine, but you abstain. Everyone is eating with gusto, you are nibbling gingerly. You try to order the most neutral dishes that will cause the least irritation, and you half-secretly take a few more Imodium tablets. It does not help. By the time dessert comes around, you are almost stationary on the toilet. The waiters only smile and the guests at your table do not even notice. You don't have dessert; when it's served you go to the toilet five more times.

Afterwards, there will be a leisurely stroll through the city. A night excursion. Everything there is to see and what they'd like to show you. You apologise that someone's waiting for you, you look at the map around the corner to see where a twnety-four hour pharmacy could be, and there is one, but it's by the railway station, which is not very close, yet you must go there, and before you get to the pharmacy, you fill your pants. There are no bars nearby, so you have to do what you have to do. You buy two packs of Imodium, immediately take two tablets and start looking for home, propping yourself up like a three-legged stool. You cannot take a taxi.

Before you arrive at your boyfriend's, you fill your pants twice more. You instantly go to the bathroom, put all your clothes in the washing machine and sit in the shower for half an hour. Your boyfriend bangs on the door, you haven't the power to answer, you mutter that everything is fine, it's nothing, and you sit under the warm water. Meanwhile, drenched and dripping, you jump three more times onto the potty. There is no end to it, there will be no end. Your stomach is utterly empty, and it keeps coming and coming.

That night you sleep between two blankets on the bathroom floor. Underfloor heating is a cruelly good thing. Your boyfriend is kind of sulky. You don't have the strength for it.

In the morning, you weigh up for a long time whether you can make it, whether your stomach can make it, and you go to the seminar. You can always leave the event. And all those people, and meh... when nothing else works, a good girl's sense of duty does. You put on two pairs of underwear and line them with toilet paper and swallow three Imodium tablets.

You drink only water. You don't even eat biscuit crumbs. You only drink water and you only go to pee. You understand that happiness is in very, very, very small things. You participate intelligently in discussions, plans are written up, and in the afternoon the participants start disappearing one by one, each on their own train or plane. You stay.

Your boyfriend is very persuasive and insists on going out to eat, no matter what, he also wants to spend time with you, he won't take no for an answer, and your stomach is seriously empty. It's been twenty-four hours since your last meal, the day has passed quite well, and until now no diarrhoea in your life has lasted longer than five days, so after such a long time, maybe you can give it a try. You snack on something. The stomach holds like it should. It's either Imodium or nature.

You get home and your clothes start to come off and

you're feeling it just now, right away, and quickly, and your boyfriend is holding you tight, and—you fill your pants before you can free yourself from your boyfriend's grasp.

You rush to the bathroom, throw all your clothes into the washing machine and head straight for the shower. You hear your boyfriend pacing back and forth down the hall. He's walking angrily, it is not a nice walk. In general, he does not practise indoor sports. Unlike you, who, has to complete your daily steps, as long as you get your numbers up. The door opens and closes. At least now you can calmly run between the room and the bathroom without feeling embarrassed.

And you run. At some point in the night, you fall asleep for a while, when you wake up, you do not know where you really are, and you fill your pants before you find the bathroom.

That is how the night passes.

Your boyfriend comes in the morning. The door opens and he stands over you and explains over and over and gets angrier and angrier and you don't understand anything because you need to run to the bathroom again. He wants to make himself clear and he clutches your arm and you need to get to the WC right now, like right now, straightaway, and he grabs you, and you fill your pants when he lets you go, and he understands, and before you can come out of the bathroom again, he's thrown your things into a suitcase, clothes, both wet and dry, and carried the suitcase to the door, and he's holding some clothes in his hand that you are supposed to put on.

You fill your pants before you get down the stairs to the front door.

My Aunt Ellen

Mudlum

I have wanted to write this story for a long time. Too long, so those memories pictured at night tend to fade over the course of days. As if what I am saying is more important than who I am talking about. It is not. The only thing that matters is who I'm talking about, even if it's barely half the truth, even if it is just a poor stream of flashbacks. Since there seems to be no one to do it but me, no one who knows Ellen, to whom she would have been so important.

Ellen is my mother's sister. There were three sisters in all, like in Chekhov. They wanted to get away in the same way, to the city, far away. Only one of them stayed on their home island and went to marry a man a few villages away. However, this story is not about her.

In the beginning, there are definitely great big inaccuracies in my story. From the time of birth, things are a bit shady. Ellen was born on 24th or 25th May, 1933. The story goes like this: when the child was born, the father was so angry that the first-born was not a son, that he went to a tavern for several days to drink, and when he eventually reached the official who registers births, he had forgotten when his daughter was born, and the wrong day was written on the birth certificate.

I do not know much about her school years, except that her grades were good, the girl was full of her own importance, could draw well and wrote poems.

The Muhu[5] attic was full of all three girls' beautiful school notebooks with calligraphic handwriting, whose back covers called on people to find and destroy invasive Colorado potato beetles. She sent her poems to a famous man from the neighboring village, Juhan Smuul, for him to read.[6] They had all been sent during Ellen's high school days. A story that lasted throughout Ellen's life and will continue in history. Although I'm not writing about Juhan, I am writing about Ellen.

How impoverished and miserably they lived, I cannot say for sure now, but I guess everyone lived more or less the same. Their father died in the first days of the war, right there in Saaremaa,[7] and was brought home to be buried, Ellen told me that she had filled in the bullet holes in the body herself. To this day, the bullet holes in our Muhu roof are still patched up with pieces of tin. A widow with three daughters, one of whom was still an infant, she had to feed and clothe them for the rest of her life. Even in the summer, when my mother went there to help with the haymaking, my grandmother took money from a green enamel jug and put it in my mother's hand—I called this jug an elephant, because it had a spout like a trunk. It is also said that their grandpapa, namely my grandfather's father (he died around '53), had harrassed the widow in a rather nasty way. I still have all kinds of letters since Ellen's death, my mother's letters to her and vice versa, and my grandmother's letters to Ellen and my mother and vice versa, but I have not wanted to read them. It doesn't seem quite right, and maybe I never will. Still, the letters that are really sought after, Juhan's letters to Ellen, I do not have those. They were said to have been hidden in a secret place in the Merivälja[8] house and they could be there; Ellen didn't destroy anything, but there they remain.

When we took possession of this house full of things after Ellen's death, no one was interested in either Ellen's writings or Smuul's papers. Since Ellen didn't give anything away after Juhan's death, an inventory of assets was written up, I guess I still have that somewhere, but no one managed to take anything away. Rumour has it that my coloured pencils are exhibited as Smuul's stationery in the Koguva museum.[9]

I had to contact the Literary Museum of Tartu myself to see if they would be interested and please, be so kind as to come and take away this pile of historically important papers—it was a huge quantity. They had these boxes used for packing TVs, and there were a lot of them. No one sorted anything either before or after that happened, so much so that I looked to make sure our family's things didn't end up there, but not very carefully.

The house was up for sale. As always, when the deceased has not made a will, there will be a terrible tussle and gnashing of teeth, and an eternal feud generated between relatives. I had kindly called the other beneficiary and asked if Smuul's materials could be given to the literary museum. I did not do it without asking permission—the answer was yes. However, some time passed, when the beneficary's son started accusing me of cheating behind their back, I had to send all kinds of letters confirming that I hadn't received a penny for it.

After finishing high school, Ellen worked for a year as a teacher in some village school—I have these lovely class pictures of her standing with the children—but then she tried to get into an art institute. She tried and got in, but without a scholarship. She studied sculpture for half a year and then dropped out of school due to lack of funds. Her next school was the University of Tartu and the subject was Estonian philology, where she was one of the first to graduate from the Finnish Language Department, and I think she got a job almost immediately in some sort of institution promoting Estonian-Finnish friendship, I don't know too much about it. It is certain, however, that she was the first Estonian language lecturer at the University of Oulu in Finland in the early '60s.

All her university abstracts, coursework, theses, the effort and fruit of a person's schoolwork, were still at Merivälja, but what one person manages to preserve in her lifetime, others manage to destroy in a single day.

Since it means nothing to anyone now.

In Tartu, Ellen also participated in some kind of acting group or amateur theatre, where she played opposite Jaan Saul,[10] there are quite a lot of photos from this period. During her university days, she was nicknamed Monga, her fellow students who came to the funeral still spoke of her as Monga, a lively, bright, intelligent girl.

It seems that her youth was quite glamorous, with well paid, important positions—she also made programmes for Finns on Estonian Television, some kind of propaganda programmes, which were then somehow distributed in Finland, there are also lavish black and white pictures of it—with her hair in curls and bright costumes. These dazzling costumes were my childhood ideal, possibly the source of my love for glittery, embroidered flashy things. I put them on one after the other, '60s mini-skirts which were full-length gowns on me. One was a kind of white brocade, with bows like silver tinsel on a Christmas tree woven into it—and like cat's whiskers, they stuck out of the fabric. Then there was a very chic black dress with thick silver lace ribbons and a particularly beautiful black crepe taffeta floral embroidered dress covered all over with pearls—she had made it herself, it was terribly, terribly beautiful.

I could painstakingly describe all the clothes that hung in her closet, all the buttons in the button boxes, the scarves in the scarf boxes, and the gloves in the glove boxes. In the glove box were long turquoise nylon gloves, white driving gloves made of soft leather, with string backs, and white bridal gloves with the texture of human skin, they were bought for Juhan and Ellen's wedding, but that wedding never came to pass.

As far back as I can remember, she was no longer working anywhere. By that I mean that she worked, but at home. She was a typist at the Perioodika publishing house.[11] If no one else can recall, a typist used the editor's red-inked proofs to enter the words cleanly on a typewriter. Perioodika published all kinds of things, calendars, cookbooks, and occasionally she also translated something from or into Finnish. She translated Rudolf Sirge's *The Land and the People*[12] into Finnish—*Maa ja kansa*, a neverending thick brick, standing at the top of the stairs on a red shelf of books in Finnish, its cover pale blue and salad green.

Ellen had two typewriters, a bigger Olympia and a cute little Baby Hermes with light green keys. I typed on that one. All kinds of things. In the beginning, only iiiiiiiii and ksölkldkjj, but then we did a book of poems, with pictures and everything, and somehow my aunt managed to give me the impression that I did it all myself, even though the poems were written by her and she helped with half of the pictures. It is still there.

We did all kinds of things together, I got all my craft skills from her. She taught me to crochet and knit, and how to knit the right way by casting the yarn over your finger like old women do, not hooking it like they teach in school. She taught me to sew and how to stitch the pieces together, and to always press the seams afterwards, and tie the threads. She taught me to hold the thread together when embroidering, and to work like in the old days in Muhu, so that only a small row of dots remains on the bad side, and to hide all the ends of the thread so that the wrong side is just as beautiful as the right, and how to use an embroidery frame. Only the use of a thimble could not be instilled in me. I can make patterns by poking holes in a plastic sheet with a needle and later apply it onto fabric using toothpaste through the holes.

We made a Puss in Boots for me, the body was made using the inner part of some sweatpants, with leopardprint leather boots and sequins up the side. A foam rubber hat and feather that kept its shape quite gallantly, a leather cape and a golden belt. I was thrilled! Then a few years later we fashioned a great Pirate with a pink body made of sheets—we dyed the cloth ourselves—with a sailor's shirt, the stripes of which I drew carefully with an ink pen, thick wool for hair, and he wore breeches and a red shawl and a gold earring, with an eyepatch over his eye, and we cut real wood for his wooden shoes with red leather buckles nailed with gold buttons!!! The pirate also had a furry vest with a purple silk border. It added up to a number of days full of interesting activities. Once I crocheted a big bag for myself—first we chose different coloured pieces of woollen cloth, crocheted multi-colored lace around each one, then I sewed the pieces together and twisted the threads into a handle. The lining was set in, everything was so incredibly neat and masterfully done. For the rest of my life, I will remember the smoky air of her upstairs bedroom, mixed with the steam of ironed woollen cloth, and the sun through which the smoke swirls—a cigarette was constantly between her teeth, and she blew the smoke and slurred out of the corner of her mouth.

I was with her most of the school holidays. In the winter, it was cold in that damned big house, and sleeping was arranged in such a way that at least five or six blankets were piled on top of you, a checkered shawl on top of a blue-flowered woollen blanket, then some kind of cotton blanket, then a few more shawls—I remember them all, one was mohair with natural dyes brought from Finland—or an angora blanket, in deep blue, dark green and dark brown tones. But what I liked most was the label in the corner, and not the right side of the label, which said a hundred per cent wool, but the wrong side, where the silk threads formed a shiny multi-coloured crest of pointy mountains.

It was cold in the mornings, and we had to descend the stairs to be in front of the stove in the warm kitchen. Next to the stove there was a seat with a backrest with a liftable cover, and you could stretch out in a crooked position there. I loved doing dishes at her place because she had a fancy stainless steel double sink and a whole set of kitchen cabinets covered in stainless steel plate. It was always insanely dirty. I liked scrubbing it all clean and washing the cabinet doors. You should have seen the pantry! There were twenty-year-old cans of Globus peas on the shelves, and her own terrible preserves, which were mostly pretty awful, containing apples, chokeberries, and cherry plums. All kinds of glass jars later replaced hundreds of empty Voimix butter boxes, there were Christmas ornaments and empty woodchip flower baskets and my old children's phone that could be used to talk between two rooms. Later, when she was really screwy, when she lived without water and electricity, there was a variety of foods in varying degrees of decomposition.

The kitchen and her upstairs bedroom, they were lived in, and they were in a crazy mess. All the other living spaces in the house, however, remained in an unchanged state for decades—where a vase stood in 1970, it still stood in 2000. The furniture stayed where it was, the books exactly where they always were, and I was allowed to read everything and take it with me to Paide, but I always put everything back in the same place. The clothes hung in the wardrobes in the same spot for decades, from time to time she re-sewed something or made two things into one, or filled in a hole somewhere, but these things always had their own story, you knew what it had been before.

Of the books, I looked at the pictures at first, there were a few shelves of art books with pictures, the Louvre and the Tretyakov Gallery and Picasso and Matisse and all sorts of others, I looked at them all, there were beautiful Finnish magazines with Hellas chocolate ads inside, and one with particularly nice pictures of Australian nature. I looked at the animal atlases and 'General History' book plates and anywhere that had pictures inside. Then I started reading, at first the adventure stories from the land and the sea,[13] then all kinds of other things that we didn't have at home, Jaan Oks[14] and expatriate Estonians and poetry books from the first Estonian republic, Smuul had acquired himself a beautiful, good library. 'The Library of Creation'[15] was in the second outer entrance, on shelves specially built for them. It was quite something.

We always went there for New Year's Eve, when she decorated the house in a most lavish way. Mobile crowns of straw were hung to celebrate the New Year, and in the living room there was a large fir wreath with candles suspended from the ceiling, and all the tables and tops were full of small bouquets of twigs, tinsel, and baubles. There was no door between the two large ground floor rooms, just a wide opening where curtains on rails had probably been planned, but at Christmas time there was full-length sparkling Christmas tree tinsel, Christmas tree rain, that's probably what it was called. There was a fire in the fireplace and everything was so beautiful.

Yet this beauty was always accompanied by fear. We never knew what my aunt's mental state was at any given moment, whether it was good, average, crazy or really crazy. Since I had already understood as a small child, and was with my mother when both an ambulance and the police had to be called for her at the same time. Sometimes she would not let us inside, we had to sneak around the house and pound on the windows and negotiate.

You stand in front of a dark house on New Year's Eve and you feel scared.

*

At that time, when I was little, Ellen had long hair. Cut those wretched long locks, my mother always told her. She wore them in a bun, with an interesting accessory such as a mesh crafted from thick white insulating wire, and to make the bun look more formidable, she had padded her hair out, and sewn it into a stocking.

The hair was wrapped around the padded part, and the ends were positioned between two wires and secured with hairpins.

Later on, she cut off her long hair, it was dark brown, slightly curly, rough, thick, and mixed with grey. She always cut it herself. She visited the city a few times a year, and then she took a taxi. No matter how poor she was, she never held back. Ten cutlets were bought, a large ice cream purchased.

I was able to eat that half a kilo by myself. When she went to town, she wore either a pink Crimplene suit or a snow-white one with silver threads, and I later used the leftovers to make a skimpy bikini for myself.

Generally, she did not go anywhere except to the shop on the hill. In the Perioodika publishing days, she still had to go to collect her salary once a month, in later years that was no longer the case, and so she didn't go there either. When she did not go to collect the money, it was understood that her illness had worsened. A man named Mikhailov from the publishing house called my mother in Paide and said that the situation with Ellen must be like this again, since she hadn't come for her wages. Then we had to go to Tallinn and find out how things were. If she was sick, we had to call the ambulance to take my aunt to the hospital. We had to carefully hide ourselves somewhere behind the corner of the shed at that time, because otherwise the relationship would have been destroyed. Of course, she guessed who had organised her hospital trips, but she probably did not want to think about it.

A hospital stay usually lasted two months, I think her physician is still practising, so I will not mention her name. She was a classic kind of powerful Jewish woman. Eventually, the medicines did their job and she was sent home. But Ellen had pets! Mother had to go from Paide to Tallinn to take care of them.

For a while, she continued to take her medicine at home, but then she would stop, and everything started all over again. She had to be put into therapy once or twice a year. Of course, that was before the blessed Republic of Estonia returned. Here, each person's health is their private matter, no one is forcibly hospitalised, and the boundaries between whether a person is dangerous to him or herself or others were and are very blurred. So, she spent the last decade or so of her life in a gloomy, difficult state of mind, interacting with people less and less, communicating only in an extremely sarcastic way, punctuated by silent pauses and teeming with insinuations. She made her handicrafts in the dark, by candlelight. After the electricity and water had been cut off to the house, she settled down in a small room next to the kitchen, whose window opened onto the terrace with the open fireplace, which was a dark place in itself, but not dark enough for Ellen, who covered the window with a black garbage bag so that not one beam of light could enter the room. In that room she had a bed, a small low table and a cupboard, no other things went in there. In its day, this room was intended as an anteroom for the sauna.

The central heating system had long since given out, the whole house was cold and unheated for years, she warmed the stove with the leftover coal from the boiler, and burnt the stove with it, somehow patched up from the inside with some kind of sheet metal. Water was taken from melted snow, in the summer she drew it from a particularly suspicious outside well and boiled it, she made candles out of old pieces of wax, but she still had to buy those. She never complained.

A few years before she died, she received an enormous amount of money from a land sale, with which she did not pay off her debts, but bought loads of badminton shuttlecocks, sets of knives and forks in suitcases, and other strange things that are sold in the Select catalogue. I remember the shuttlecocks the most vividly. She also had a mood ring, a Peter the First Faberge Easter egg, and a pile of leather jackets made of patches, a huge one later went to Reedik, a slightly smaller one is still worn by my mother, Ellen herself faithfully wore a patchwork vest, and there were more bags of various sizes filled with all sorts. For the most part, everything was still in its cellophane packaging, towels and strange silk ersatz table runners and weird plastic boxes with baroque decorations. She acquired a big jar of clear preservative from somewhere and poured it over her jams to preserve them even more. Shuttlecocks, which I cannot get over or around, were on the pantry shelf, forty to fifty of them.

She had been very careful with her money, so her heirs got most of it.

Ellen was a master of recycling. She not only collected everything, pull tabs from tin cans, ends of thread, silver foil from cigarette packs, milk cartons, oddly shaped roots, shells, pots, driftwood from the beach, but also used them to make all kinds of things. The ends of threads went into pillow stuffing, she embroidered and dyed all her own sewing threads from garments that had previously unravelled, using them over and over to make rugs, pillows, and clothes from rags using the applique technique. Jumpers were made from untangled yarns, which she had dyed herself and wound together with a spinning wheel, one yarn consisted of several threads of different shades, and her knits were real masterpieces, with subtle transitions of colours, there were always some embroideries somewhere. Broken things were repaired with embroidered flowers, worn elbow patches were crocheted.

In terms of clothes, she never stopped caring throughout her life, even though she lived alone, she did not go anywhere, what she covered her body with was always tastefully chosen, she often changed outfits several times a day, she had her special clothes for stoking the boiler or other dirty work, clothes for working in the garden, and clothes for going shopping. In later years, she mostly wore homemade stirrup trousers, she had many different pairs, from light beige and white to black. Her clothes were always ironed. If the laundry was too dried out, it was rolled up in a damp bed sheet, carefully pressed and properly hung from a hanger.

Anyone who has bothered to read this long story will wonder why I am not talking about Smuul. The main reason? I do not know much about him and it doesn't really matter to me, but it did to Ellen. I associate Juhan the most with a cup that had a purple rat, a green cat and a monkey on it. It was called the Varvara Monkey Cup because Juhan had had a monkey named Varvara on board ship during his voyage to Africa. I drank cocoa from that cup. When the cup broke, the damage was great, and the pieces were kept. Of course, the air was thick with Juhan, he was everywhere, on the walls, on the pictures, on the bookshelves, his death mask and death hand were in the study, he was in people's stories and allusions. At school, a female classmate told me that her mother had heard how Juhan had pleaded with Ellen—give me a child! It must have been when Ellen still lived in the apartment on Endla Street and Juhan visited her. Either there was a colossal argument or the walls were exceptionally thin—I do not know where the truth is, I only know small fragments and scraps of stories, and they are all mixed up in my head.

It is commonly held that the story went like this. Having sent poems to Smuul during her school days, they remained in correspondence, with infrequent meetings over a long period. They started living together when Ellen was about thirty-four years old. I have no idea which men, relationships and things could fit in between. For Ellen, there was only one man she recognised, and that was Juhan. Vaarandi[16] was six years older than Smuul, and Ellen was eleven years younger, I am not even going to check that. In all kinds of circles, Ellen is probably resented for not controlling Juhan's excessive drinking, but happily got drunk with him. They bought the house from Edgar Tõnurist[17] and registered it in Ellen's name, because even a Lenin Prize laureate was not allowed to own two houses. Of course, Debora got the house on Kuristiku Street, and the Volga car too. And Ellen didn't receive the royalties, she only got the house. And she persevered bravely in this, although she was forbidden to sell, but she claimed that the Smuul Museum would one day be there, and continued her path of suffering. During the house renovations, they allegedly liquored up their builders with cognac and everything was done in a hurry, once they even singed the parquet floor, and the construction was left unfinished. After Juhan's death, Ellen fell from a great height. Apparently, she started drinking even worse until my mother took her to rehab. As far as I know, she stayed sober for the rest of her life. However, alcoholism channelled into schizophrenia.

The core of her delusion was briefly as follows: after the war, it was said that the family hid two Nazi criminals, Laak and Gerretz, on our farm. Ellen had recognised them. Henceforth, she was the subject of relentless pursuits, assassination attempts and wiretapping. Every event in her life was somehow positioned in this scheme. There was a supposedly suspicious bicycle accident that took place while she was out visiting, a few car accidents she'd had of the same nature, she also showed me the dents on the gold bracelet given to her by President Kekkonen,[18] which had occurred during the accident. When she wanted to tell me something important, we went to the balcony because the house was said to be full of listening and watching devices. There was a wooden box at the end of the phone line, a screen in front of the TV.

From time to time she suspected that her food was poisoned and did not eat much for long periods. Encrypted messages intended personally for her were broadcast on television, and she would read all kinds of clues from any newspaper she could get her hands on. She was a communist, but the kind of communist who knew that the country was prejudiced, that things were not moving in the right direction, that everything was being controlled and all the threads were held together by someone's invisible secret plan. She wrote long reports about it and sent them out far and wide, right up to the Central Committee.

It is very difficult to describe this disease, it was extremely uniform on the one hand and enormouly variable on the other. Martin remembers collecting the skin that peeled off her hands in one big pile, it was all from the radiation, she said. It was her tone of voice that signalled that things were going to get worse. Her voice became very low and speaking was slowed by longer and longer pauses. There were extended silences where she became pensive, and suddenly an abrupt and violently presented train of thought would burst forth. Walking became creeping. There was virtually nothing that we would dare speak about to her any more, because she could find something sinister in everything, absolutely everything. There were no things that were not suspicious. The highlight of the day was listening to the news, she always listened to it very intently in her armchair, hunched forward, a cigarette in the corner of her mouth, when no one was allowed to say a thing, Ellen immediately said very malevolently: shush!

Of course, Juhan's death was murder, no matter what kind or how, though in my childhood I could not comprehend this.

She was intolerant of the films that were made with Smuul's material, she did not tolerate anything in general. But when she was in a period of recovery, at times she even admitted that some of her thoughts were flawed. At the moment, I am thinking that such a schizophrenic world view is not directly more skewed or incorrect than any other kind of perception of life, but it is certainly very difficult to bear. Excruciatingly difficult. Besides myself and my mother, she did not really get along with anyone, not much with the neighbours, everyone knew how things were, and Ellen herself was a complete misanthrope. The older I got, the less she tolerated me, especially the men in my life, and she was totally right about that. But she loved Martin. Maybe as much as me when I was little, maybe more. Children were not the tools of evil... in the end, I was too busy living my own life, I rarely went to Merivälja, I sat on the kitchen table for half an hour, Ellen showed me the rugs she had embroidered in the meantime, when she was in a brighter mood, when she was in a worse mood, the oppressive, evil silence just had to be endured. She still offered a cup of coffee, the coffee was always on the stove and I think the pot was never washed, and its sides were caked with a centimetre's thickness of hairy, greasy coffee residue. Yet Martin visited her more often, and after Ellen's death I found several messages in the house that she had left just in case—Martin, I'm out at the shop on the hill, or I went to Pirita or Miiduranna.

Ellen's garden was an attraction in itself. I have forgotten how many different kinds of trees and bushes grew there, maybe seventy? Along the path leading to the door there was laburnum and dark pink hawthorn and a beautiful soft fir tree, a great, old oak tree grew under the window of my room. The room was a little dark because of that, but there is nothing more beautiful than the rustle of oak branches outside the window, blowing with the wind against the tin roof. There was an old curved elm that had spread itself over the roof of the cellar, under which we buried my dog, there was a spruce hedge behind the house, a big, mature horse chestnut by the garage lane and a huge Douglas fir, always full of cones. There were plum trees with yellow and purple plums and this horrible cherry plum and chokeberry bush and redcurrants and gooseberries, and some old apple trees that didn't bear very well, but standing right by the house, so the branches reached the balcony, there was a yellow transparent apple tree, good and sweet. Many kinds of cypresses, Savin junipers, mountain pines, various yews, birches, well, it was one beautiful garden. And everywhere along the edges of the garden periwinkle grew with its blue flowers. There was lily of the valley in shady places and daisies in the grass.

There was a big pond, where ducks ate up the water lilies, but the bulrushes persisted, and even some fish lived there, though I really do not know how that is possible.

Although we pottered about in the garden, in earlier years Ellen herself did not bother to do anything there, Mum used to mow, in the spring we raked leaves and carried them to the fire in an old great bed sheet. The grass was so full of moss, once they wanted to shoot a Miss Marple film in her garden, it would make a beautiful English lawn, but of course Ellen didn't allow it. Later she started to like tinkering outside and then, when she was deeply impoverished, she made her own ground elder soup with egg, very tasty! She grew a few strawberries, weeded her little rock garden, but she did not like mowing the lawn. Just before her death, she finally bought a decent lawnmower, before that everything was done with a scythe.

When the house was sold, which is such an awful story that I will not tell it here, I didn't visit the place for years. Until one time I looked at 13 Kesk Street on Google Maps and saw a strange, big, grey square. And I went to see. Regardless of who bought it, or whoever has resold it in the meantime, the garden has been destroyed, the house torn down and a concrete cube the size of the whole plot has been built on it, it looked very unfinished when I saw it. I will never go there again.

*

It is a beautiful spring outside, and it seems that a little more gloomy weather is needed for an Ellen story. Dear readers, rejoice, this will be the last. Photos will not appear here at all, someday, when time has restored access to cardboard boxes with pictures inside, maybe I will do a separate retrospective. There are images whose very existence is gut-wrenching. I have photos of Ellen in the hospital, she had a camera with her and she took a picture of the old man in the next bed and asked for pictures of herself when she was in intensive care, tubes writhing around her. I do not know what to do with them, throw them away or burn them, but I cannot do that because of old superstitious customs, but they do give off a horrible smell of death.

Ellen celebrated her seventieth birthday on her terrace with the open fireplace, in the same beautiful spring as right now. Then in August, she called me to come and see her, saying that she was not feeling well. We went there to talk for several days, and Martin and I bought her a mobile phone in Pirita so that she could get in touch quickly. The paramedics did not want to come, and this ambulance officer was one scary-bitch mamma, she told her to go to the family doctor, and she asked what was wrong. And there was nothing more wrong other than death, which came two weeks later.

She liked the hospital. She gave me her packs of cigarettes, said she didn't want them any more. It was warm and white on the ward, there was nothing that had to be done. The orderlies gave her a warm shower. My mother had already moved to live in Muhu, I was the only one in town, I went to see her in the hospital for a couple of days with my little daughter, and on those days when I wasn't in the hospital, I went to Merivälja to feed the cat. Mum promised to take the cat, but a more practical relative tied a brick under its stomach and threw it into the pond. Quite a difficult combination, with my work and my child in the nursery and all that wasted effort, I was furious about that cat being drowned! Once the sisters came up from the country, you know those embarrassing moments around the sick bed, nobody really knows how to talk about anything or do anything, until Ellen said now it's time to go. And of course, is it so bad that you had to come? Nor did she want to die. She didn't have that thought in mind. We didn't ask for an autopsy, it was known that she was riddled with cancer, and whose business is it to know exactly where it all began.

After her death, the house was empty for two years, the urn on the downstairs bookcase, and finally buried in the Muhu cemetery, where our plot is, even though Ellen wanted to be with Juhan. The ashes could have been put there. She also had a little bag wrapped in silver foil in the closet, which contained some soil from the Forest Cemetery[19] and some of Juhan's fingernails, but I could no longer find it.

Mudlum: I've dreamed of Ellen two nights in a row and this house and in many, many recurring dreams I have seen her die only to wake up in a coffin and live happily ever after, and no one received any inheritance.

Martin: I remember one of these dreams in great detail.

Mudlum: And I have dreamed many times that she sold the house, but those who bought it don't live there, and one can still visit.

Do you remember my dream? And today I saw her out there in the front hallway going to sweep the leaves off the path, but she went through the wall. Then I screamed a little and woke up.

Martin: Yes, I remember your dream, you told it well.

Mudlum: Hmm, anyway I dreamed it again.

Martin: I wonder if it was the same?

Mudlum: Hardly, this time the coffin was outside in front of the very same house, by the corner of the garage. She opened her eyes nicely in the coffin and started doing her Ellen thing again and everyone stared dumbfounded, waiting for her to die again. But she did not die.

There must have been some years when I did not think about it too much, not in reality, not in my dreams. But then they started coming. Places. Ellen and the place were one. The place is always the same, but Ellen is a little different, such layers of time on top of each other, sometimes I see her as she was in my childhood, sometimes I see her as she was in her later years, sometimes as she never was. But always right there, nowhere else. In her own house. This house has become a symbol of time, a place where all things come together, all thoughts and memories, they are there at the same time, like thin sheets of cigarette paper on top of each other, the lower ones shining through the upper ones. Maybe not a symbol of time, it's not the right word either, maybe time itself or a place where things are as if there is no time. I don't know, it's too complicated a thought for me. I feel it, but I cannot speak it.

I can see my room, upstairs, behind the oak tree, it was always dark and cool. I look out of the window. I do not see it in my mind's eye, but I *am* there. So, what is reality if not a memory that has stored every light, shadow, smell, sound, feeling, colour, footsteps behind the door, a cat's pawing on the tin roof, the roughness of a blanket, the colour and texture of sheets. There was one tiny red pillow, it had a '60s pattern, yellow and red striped spots. And how big is the world, if every head contains a world of lost things, that world is precisely as big as a memory can stretch. In other words, maybe no more than a hundred years. A small world. Small, but terribly broad, because if you put together the memories of all the heads, it will be a thicker book in a hundred years than there have been days since the beginning of the world.

I see myself in that downstairs room, which was even darker, even smaller, next to the hallway, with little Martin, Ellen had bad days then, and for some weeks she never came to see us. A nurse, who was sent to check the living conditions of infants, wrote in her papers: Unsatisfactory. I walked back and forth in the big room at night, the baby in my arms, the quiet, the unlit house, the fear, we weren't permitted to cry. Not me, not the baby.

Then came the days full of sun, there was no one who could love a new person more, who marvelled at his stories, kept all his drawings, every word scribbled somewhere. In the end, she crocheted and knitted wonderful jumpers and slippers for him, kept a stock of chocolates at home. Maybe she intended for Martin to play badminton.

Ellen—this is the whole world. It is so interesting, I am terribly sorry that I don't remember more, better, more accurately her stories, sayings, jokes. I still remember myself in the middle of things where she was in the centre. But this I say, there was none brighter, wittier, sharper, more generous than Ellen in her good days. But her bad days gave my world another dimension.

Bigger, deeper, higher—the size of a giant.

The Women's Sauna

Mudlum

It is undeniable that public saunas have fallen into historical
obscurity. There are certainly some still left, and there are
probably people who cannot nurture their bodies elsewhere.
But most people who used to go to the sauna have now
accumulated enough wealth that they have converted their
closet into a shower room. I even know an apartment where a
real Finnish sauna was built in a pantry or utility room, and most
likely they did not put much effort into moisture protection.
Every blessed sauna day, which always coincided with a
bigger party, they drowned their downstairs neighbours with
festive carelessness. Then an angry neighbour in tracksuit and
slippers comes there and is greeted with effusive friendliness
by a whole group of hot, naked, steaming guys, some with

sauna towels wrapped around their hips, and they invite the quarrelsome citizen inside. He is offered good things, the vodka bottle is passed around, and look, it won't be long before the man is willing to throw off his tracksuit and climb into the sauna! It was probably that Volodya fixed their pipes badly or something like that had happened. It was a cool apartment, one room as big as an old manor hall, and no superfluous junk cluttering up the place. In the middle of the room, with its back to the long windowsill, stood a saggy Finnish leather sofa. In front of it was an improvised table, an old door on bricks, and on the table all of life's necessities, enough drinks to satisfy an entire regiment of dragoons, heaps of salted nuts and other snacks to nibble. There was a washing machine in the corner of the kitchen, and on top of the washing machine was a state-of-the-art ceramic hob. Why have furniture when you have so much space that you can spread all your worldly possessions over the floor, one by one? In the bedroom there was a wide mattress on the floor and that was it. Clothes were stored in large sports bags. A clothesline ran across a room that was bigger than some other people's entire property.

People who build Finnish saunas in their own apartments risk damaging their neighbours' property because of poor construction. However, I know that municipal saunas have caused the same trouble. Namely, there was once such a sauna house in the city centre, where there had been a sauna on the first floor since the tsarist era, while the other floors housed the living quarters of the wealthier people. For a good eighty years, the sauna steam disintegrated the structure of the building, until one day the legs of a male citizen appeared from the ceiling of the women's bathroom, he had sunk through the floor. With the restoration of Estonian independence,[20] this sauna underwent all kinds of metamorphoses, first it was an upstanding institution, but then a small number of saunas that could be hired by the hour started to appear, the former washrooms turned into a drunkards' corner, where downtrodden neighbours could quietly sip their cognac. Since it must be dark in a bar for faces to look their most attractive, the windows were covered with black curtains and the only element of beauty was a large colourful aquarium glowing in the darkness, shimmering green and mysterious, the fish swimming in their cubic water world and looking directly into another dimension with their googly eyes. I have always been fascinated by aquariums, they are found, for example, in children's polyclinics and other respectable public places as a sign of ultimate luxury, the sight of fish supposedly calms nervous people, I wonder if fish are also calmed by looking at anxious humans? How do you just hoist up a bunch of non-terrestrial life forms in a glass box somewhere along a corridor wall?

Well, I wanted to talk about saunas. When I was very small, my mother and I went to the city sauna. We had nowhere to wash at home. I remember it like it was yesterday. The sauna room was dark and so hot that a little flea like me was sitting on the lowest step, while somewhere under the dim ceiling, big, respectable matrons were enthroned and beating each other with birch whisks. An incredibly large stove was alight in the corner, on which the old crones kept pouring water from a cup, and then it hissed! How they scrubbed and rubbed themselves, their big bellies and tiny feet, cleanliness was a completely different concept at that time, it cannot be compared with today's customs. I think they almost flayed themselves. First, of course, a visitor to the sauna had to check if there were any free benches at all and carefully glide to the spot without slipping on a floor covered with soap bubbles. Sometimes there were no bowls available to use, they were made of galvanised zinc, some were bright white like fresh herring, but others were blackish grey from age and a little dented. They smelled very metallic. It was necessary to provide two bowls, one for the feet. With a bowl in hand, you went to the taps, which were at the end of long pipes painted red and blue respectively, and these pipes shook when the white tap was turned, and the water shot out with such pressure as if the whole contraption could blow up in an instant. The water from the cold tap was as freezing as if it had come from a hole in the ice, and the blue pipe above it was covered with tiny bubbles of steam, along which ran fine rivulets of condensed water. The red hot water pipe, on the other hand, was glowing, and if you dared to touch the tap at all, water of more than a hundred degrees came out of it and it sprayed in a big arc like a fountain, so you had to keep a good distance from both the bowl and the tap if you did not want to risk burns. I don't understand how people survived the sauna at all. Firstly, that same boiling water was placed into a bowl, then that full bowl was rinsed over the stone bench, so that those nearby took care to ensure that their feet would not be scalded. Whitish turbid rivulets flowed on the floor and there was a smell of honest soap, such a scent no longer exists today, except, of course, in homes with soap still in storage, because no one could use up as much of it as was acquired in the old days. I have a feeling that this soap was yellowish white, with мыло[21] written on it, and it did not lather, it was just slippery. Some show-offs might have strawberry soap that was pink and sweet-smelling and wrapped in paper so pretty it couldn't be thrown away, little red strawberries on smooth white paper, and you could sniff it endlessly.

It also seems to me that the shampoo had 'shampoo' written on it, and that it was dark brown like beer, in a horizontally striped plastic bottle that is a bit thinner in the middle like a curvaceous lady. Your head was rinsed with vinegar water, although not in the sauna, though vinegar was probably not taken in there. Yet nothing was more delicious than licking the faintly sour water flowing over your face, your eyes tightly closed, with Mum continually pouring the vinegar on your head so that your hair would be clean and smooth. 'Hair is clean when it scrunches under your finger,' she said, and pulled my hair.

Of course, it is nice when your mum washes your head. Disgusting, but nice. Some people never learn how to wash their head throughout their life. I have heard of boys who had some sort of rubber ring put on their head while washing their hair, sort of like the edge of a flying saucer, to keep the soap out of their eyes. I myself have not seen such a crown, but I believe in its existence, because all kinds of things have been invented, I remember something like a potty toilet-seat-helper, so that tiny tots can also use the toilet without falling into the hole. Well, what did I want to say? That some people do not learn how to wash their heads. One man had his wife wash his head when his mother stopped doing it. Yes! She washed it! He held his hand in front of his forehead like a visor so that the water wouldn't fall into his eyes, with his other hand he brushed his thin black hair, which was like cotton wool, fluffy and fluttering about. Without outside help, and a caring, guiding hand, some people would remain very unclean! They were probably scrubbed as children by that powerful type of women who scour themselves to a deep clean in the sauna. First, you should wash lightly, just soap yourself and rinse with water. After that, you should climb onto the bench where you can anoint yourself with mysterious home-made concoctions comprising table salt, soda, honey, and God knows what else. Rubbing with salt in the steam room is considered a means of losing weight. On their heads the matrons wear large turbans of wrapped towels to keep their hair from falling down in the heat, while beneath the towels, their hair and head were smeared with the creams and potions they had made up in their witch's kitchen at home. When they leave the sauna fiery red, they take an ice-cold shower to cheer themselves up and dash straight back to the dark, hot cave. Sometimes there are so many people on the benches that it looks as if big geese are sitting very close together, the lower benches are a little more sparsely populated, but there were enough mamas on all three levels, like a photo for a class or choir, with the rows artistically arranged.

Thus, after three or four stints of invigorating yourself with fluctuating temperatures, you finally began to really wash. After such treatment, all the dirt and dead skin had already been dislodged from the body and rolled onto the floor. (I was checked in the same way during drying: 'Well, is there any dead skin?' If the rollers ran smoothly along the skin while drying with a towel, the cleansing was complete). Then they took a powerful loofah and began to scrub everywhere, so that the sponge blazed like lightning, and the body felt so tender. From head to toe, and woah! a bowl full of water was poured on your back and it started again. Your feet were soaking all this time in a bowl of hot water and by the end were as soft and red as boiled beetroot. Finally, the soles were scoured with terrifying files, scrapers and pumice stones. The women heaved their large breasts and rubbed them up and down as if to cleanse their souls. Their heads foamed and their brows furrowed, with soapy suds they scrubbed inside and behind their ears, every last millimetre of skin, every crease and in between their toes was rubbed over a hundred times. Maybe for the sake of this sacred body-scraping ritual, they took a longer break between bathing and let the dirt build up, but maybe that was just the fashion back then. Today, I know people who never pick up a sponge, they just put a little shower gel on their hands and gently slide it over their bodies, the mild warm water and soft foam enveloping and pampering them. A sponge is considered too rough and able to chafe the skin. Even if you take a shower every morning, you will not need soap to get clean. Not to mention lounging in the bath, a glass of wine next to you and a book in your wet hands, a cloud of foam rising to the sky. And all this time, the water is quietly added, so that as long as new bubbles appear and the water doesn't cool down, they do not care about nature or how many cubic metres they need to pay for, they keep buying bath balls, fragrant oils and purple coloured salt. They can go to the bath at any hour, if they only think of it, at midnight or noon, but in the old days you had to stand in line for several hours to get into the sauna, you would be happy when you were so close to the gate of the temple of purity that you could rest your arse on those three chairs reserved for those waiting. A portly auntie sold sauna tickets, sauna whisks, and lemonade from a small booth. After visiting the sauna, you could get the lemonade to drink in the changing room, wrapped in a towel, it was so good! And when several sections of the queue had already been passed, which started outside the door, there was further waiting for a bowl or a bench, in the shower line (because one or two of them were always broken), then in the dressing room the women waited to use the big UFO-like hair dryer that grew out of the back of a brown chair. After all, you cannot go outside with a wet head in the middle of frosty weather. Household hair dryers, when there were some, were also big like monsters, we had a white one that whirred horribly, with a long red tube at the end of the fan, which ended in a puffy hat. It was probably intended so you could extend the dryer; in any event, you twisted the hair rollers on your head, put the hat on and sat for a few hours with your head inside the wind. I played being an elephant with a very long red trunk with that hat. Beauty accessories still remind me of the hair rollers, they were small things that had to be kept in hot water, they were probably full of candle wax in the middle, and they were attached to the head with white plastic caps that did not hold anything in place, but maybe I invented this device just now on the spot. In a word, the women are sitting there half-clothed, their heads inside the dome, the hot wind is blowing all around them, the sauna lady goes in from time to time to mop up the moisture from the floor with a cloth, big and small, young and old women are bustling about everywhere, putting on woollen trousers, lacing their boots, clipping their bra hooks together. The dirty clothes are folded up, then fresh, clean pink or light blue underwear of Egyptian cotton are put on. From time to time, the screaming of women can be heard from the changing room, I guess some arsehole has again tried to peek in at the ladies through the window ventilation, and someone has drenched him with a bucket of water in his face.

Finally, the sauna users have finished, the last dead skin is rubbed off with linen towels, the body's renewal can begin. The old ladies sit surrounded by their soap boxes, wash rags, tangled stockings, cotton bras, tiny tots shine with cleanliness, mothers button their shirts and pull jumpers over their heads, comb their hair, tie the ribbons on their hats. Some come, others go, the sauna stove is always hot, the door glass is covered in icicles and a wee white moon is shining in the sky, as contented clean feet are crunching their way through the snowy city streets. At home, they spread out wet sheets to dry, drink tea and eat bread with jam.

For a long time, we had no washing facilities in the countryside. In the summertime, the tin tub was simply taken outside, and the water was placed in the sun. Behind the lilac bush, all the most important procedures could be carried out, a little hot water was boiled indoors and carried out with a bucket. A good warm blend was mixed into a mug, and the great sloshing started. A towel hung from a branch, the peonies smelled fragrant, every now and then a chunky horsefly landed on someone's bare thigh. Washing also took place in the sea, at sunset, when the water is the warmest, the womenfolk walked through the pastures, soap and rolled towels tucked under their arms. Of course, you should not make seawater soapy, should you? There are small sticklebacks by the shore, we pass by them and go behind the nook of a thicket of reeds, a little further on there is a big flat stone where we can put our soap, and thus, knee-deep in water, we start to wash ourselves. The air is cool, the women have goosebumps, but the water is dark and warm. The blush of the setting sun spreads across the horizon, smelling of summer and silence. Maidens whisking in the moonlight, like in a fairy tale, serenely come up from the sea, squat on the beach stones and dress in clothes that stick to their damp skin. To make it even more beautiful, the fragrance of butterfly orchids fills the air and the grasshoppers chirp, although the butterfly orchids' scent is detected in Midsummer and the grasshoppers' chirp is heard in August, in my mind they have come together here, in this summer pasture. We untie the hooks of the barbed wire fences, there are three of these gates on the way. Upon waking in the morning, your hair is like straw and dull, some of the soap must have been left on your head. You must rinse it with rainwater, rainwater is better than any vinegar, it's as slippery as if it were made of soap, and if there has not been a drought, there is always a supply of it in a big barrel near the corner of the house. Less bathing could be done outside under the spout, using a hand washing bowl which was nailed to the wall of the house, though I liked this thing very much and I wanted to wash my head under it, so I kept knocking the spout with the back of my head and the water splashed down my neck and ears. You couldn't really clean yourself that way, because it probably only held a couple of litres. Teeth were brushed on the outside steps with a tea glass filled with water in one hand, a brush in the other, and rinse water was spat out onto the grass in a splash. The bristles of the toothbrush must have come from a pig, hard and yellow and matted in the middle, but the paste tasted like orange.

Mudlum

I know a young genius who does not set any conditions for life other than that he should have a bath in his home. Namely, he thinks in the bath, as Diogenes thought in the barrel. Of course, he often lives in places where there is no bath at all, as long as water comes from a tap. All his more advanced friends already know that when the man comes to visit, he must first be offered a bath. You can go on with your usual routine, he will be there for at least an hour. During stressful periods of work, he needed a bath several times a day and for several hours. A bath calms, relaxes, makes the body weightless, the hands rise to the surface like two fishing corks, the brain, on the other hand, weaves thoughts, and such new ideas, small, nimble and a bit transparent, are everywhere. When he finally climbs out of the water, he is lively and alert as a lizard in the sun. I can't stay in the bath for too long, I get dizzy and my heart starts racing. Only once I had a luxurious bathroom, like King Solomon's tomb, sparkling and iridescent, golden garlands ran along the walls, dried rosebuds floated artistically in beautiful vessels, once I even lit candles to make it just right. After ten years, I threw away those same dusty candles with a heavy heart, because I no longer had a bath, and these beautiful candles do not last long, the wick sinks into the wax. Yet my friends appreciated my romantic bathroom. They came there alone or with a partner, with or without champagne, I would be a clever fool to come up with a romantic bathing rental concept, but no, I just let them paddle about like that. Nor am I an envious person. It is quite possible that my bath has made people happy. That is enough for me. Even now, I often provide the service of a public bathing facility. I use my machine to wash the clothes of people who don't have such a household appliance, and I let anyone use the shower who expresses a desire to do so. Because I myself have been in other people's baths and washed my own clothing in other people's homes. Sure, Estonians are a tightfisted nation, but we don't prohibit anyone from washing. First, we put the sausage in the cupboard and hide the bread, but we allow water in abundance. Not a single villager would forbid a traveller to drink from his well. The host himself brings a bowl and a towel if the guest wants to wash his feet. So, there they are sitting at the kitchen table, one with his trouser legs rolled up and his feet in the water, while the other carefully pours a bowl of hot water for him.

Sometimes, however, taking a bath is not very pleasant, for example, in one house there was a large and opulent bathroom with a black and white tiled floor, but the bath was so gigantic that your feet could not reach the edge of the bath if you wanted to sit there, as is often the case. It was some kind of reclining bath, or Gulliver's own, the big Gulliver, not the ones so small that they disappear into one's pores. There was never enough hot water for such a large tub, it was about one-third full, rising slightly as the body splashed its way in. After all, cast iron baths are designed to retain heat for a long time, and yet, when they are iron cold, smothered with the chill of a cold room, they will cool down even the slightest bit of warmth very quickly. Half of the body in the lukewarm water, the other half shivering outside, trying to grab hold of something so that your arse does not slide along the bottom, it was necessary to act quickly. Swish and swash and you're done! And then immediately under three blankets to get just a little warm. Hot cocoa wouldn't go astray either.

Some people without a bathroom washed their child in the sink until he went to school! But then he could not fit in there any more. I do not know why they didn't think to get a baby bath, but they figured they had come up with a good idea and it worked. They sang this little song to him: *Wash your hands with soap! Or your life will have no hope!* The child was very happy and grew up to be a decent person. Washing tubs and vats come into vogue again, what is this barrel sauna but the same wooden trough in which Hans von Risbiter[22] had his maids wash him. Instead of a city sauna, there are now spas, such modern terms, yes, life has become better, better than good, and excessively expensive.

Sometimes, of course, you don't feel like washing yourself at all. You walk around for a week, your hair looking haggard, your collar sweaty, and you wallow in your own laziness and filth. It is also kind of nice, as if every day you become more yourself, a depressed human animal. You don't want to do anything, just lie down, you don't even change the sheets, why would you use clean bedclothes when you're dirty? With a greasy blanket over your head, you wait for the bad times to pass. You turn over and close your eyes, before yourself and the world. But then, in a more wakeful moment, you decisively remove your clothes in a cold room, look at your dirty body and black toes, and let the heat flow to your head. As long as it warms up inside, you grab an old loofah and a bar of soap and just like that, you wash and wash. Afterwards, you sit in the kitchen by the stove in a big old dressing gown, clean and happy. What more do you want from life!

The Boys in the Snow

Lilli Luuk

I am still trying to write as promised. Today is a quiet and very cold day. The snow stretches as far as you can see.

The morning was remembered as rose-tinted and crisp. A faint, unsettled February wind played with the snow that fell on the fields at night. The wind lifted the white powder from the flat fields into the air, allowed it to sparkle for a moment in the bright light of the waking sun, and then dropped indifferently on the smooth white banks. A bus full of children made two winding tracks in the new snow, skidding, and screeching around the bends of the icy gravel road.

The boy charged off the bus at the school stop with the others, sideways, elbows pressed inside his grey waterproof jacket, but when the bus stopped and turned around in the square, leaving behind the stench of oil, he was the last to join the group of rowdy children. A dark green loose sports bag, dirty underneath, books sinking down one side, beat against his thigh to the rhythm of his slow steps. His heart was beating too, but not all the way down to his boots. In fact, his brother's boots did not really have legs. They were such low boots, a bit big, but they did just fine with a woollen sock knitted by Grandma.

Regret pounded under the boy's red and blue beanie, under his strawberry-blonde hair. Why could he not tell his mother yesterday that he was sick, she wouldn't have asked for anything more, would have left him at home, would have left him even if he had just said he didn't want to go to school. It had been a good plan, the best plan to wake to in the morning, after an oppressive sleep. Buy some time. But… his mother had already left in the morning, the kitchen was chilly, bread and boiled eggs on the kitchen table, a cow giving birth on a farm, the story is complicated, a vet must always be ready to go, be it night or early morning. So, the boy had no one to ask and no backup plan, and he had to go off alone into the darkness, the usual morning darkness of winter in the countryside. To the bus stop, which was really just a post with the letter 'A' hanging off it, on the edge of an open field.

The round eyes of the bus appeared even before it sounded in the receding night, and in the frosty window the film began with landscapes of endless fields, silent forests, solitary, low cottages, milk stands and the flapping tin signs of bus stops. Kilometre by kilometre, the terrain opened up to the winter light, which despite the fact that the day was already a little longer than yesterday, could still barely gleam for even part of a school day. When the boy's lessons are over and the children around him are making a racket at the bus stop, throwing snow and the school bags of the younger pupils, the light struggles once more in the suffocating darkness.

What can I say about life here? All the days are the same. Rising early, disturbed nights. When you're on watch, you always tend to sleep.

The boy could not wait any longer at school today, couldn't wait for the daylight to give way to darkness and get home. Something had to happen before that. A miracle. The dull grey eyes of the Russian language teacher were piercing, her gaze haunted the boy in the haze of pre-sleep, bearing down closer and closer before the ringing of the bell, like the lights of the LAZ bus on a loathsome Monday morning.[23] Time inside the heartless clock spins at its own pace and will not stop for people's fears and dreams. The incessant noise of chatter and the distinctive smell of wool from patterned mittens, the scent of smoking furnaces and melting snow filled the high-ceiling cloakroom in the basement cellar of the manor,[24] until the tinny school bell, not at all tender, as promised in the song of the first day of school, cut like the blade of a screeching saw through the old cellar walls, driving the children up the stairs, from the corridors of the building extension and into the classrooms.

Square roots and squares in a notebook with blue frayed paper, whose back pages were densely filled with drawings of tanks and nuclear mushroom clouds, still gave the boy a grace period. The bright lights were on in the classroom for the first lesson, but a moment before the caretaker could schlep into the gymnasium and ring the school bell while counting the checkerboards on the floor tiles of the basement corridor, the teacher in a grey dress whose grey roots showed through her dyed hair clicked the switch next to the door with her slender fingers, and meagre daylight was allowed to pour into the classroom through the large windows. The boy slowly picked up the things from the table into his bag and let his eyes adjust.

There were no more options left for him in the green-walled hallway. Nylon backpacks, dirty and misshapen gym bags flew into a heap on the brown wooden floor under the bulletin board, and the noise obfuscated the danger in an instant. A rank stench always wafted from the open door of the boys' toilets as he passed by the rowdy group without saying a word to anyone and moved down the stairs to the cloakroom at a measured pace, accompanied by a suspicious look from behind the glasses of the caretaker. It was obviously mandatory homework for the girls' woodwork class, which sank into the folds of her blue and red checked uniform skirt, long wooden rods sticking out discouragingly at the boy. When the girl looked at her watch and the white lambswool sphere rolled onto the floor as she ran along the corridor to her practical lesson, the boy was already pulling on his black-patterned gloves at the school door and breathing in the winter air that had softened as the morning progressed. Then he turned the corner of the school building and quickly walked down the lane to the pond in the school grounds. In the middle of the pond was a small bushy island, that you reached by a dilapidated bridge, which the year eight boys frequented in the spring, when the leaves were already turning yellow on the banks of the waterways, to lounge around and smoke during recess. No need to go there right now. In the mud at the bottom of the pond there were litters of bones of unwanted puppies and kittens. Currently, the pond was covered with ice and a soft layer of nocturnal snow. The boy walked across the pond, past the island, and on the other side, with his thirteen-year-old long legs, effortlessly jumped over the snowy, crumbling stone wall. He waited for a beige Moskvich to pass, and then, inhaling the exhaust fumes with pleasure, walked obliquely across the road in the direction of the collective farm's warehouses.

To be honest, I haven't had a full night's sleep in a long time. People have come together here from very different places.

A white field of snow beckoned on the other side of the motorway. The boy had taken a shortcut across the field. The driver of a passing car could see him on the side of the road, stop and roll down the window and ask why he is not in school at this time of day, when all the children are currently setting their Russian language exercise books on their desks. Getting ready. The Russian language teacher is still standing facing the window and looking into the distance, here, towards the fields. It's as if she has forgotten the class, her dark pixie cut sinking forward over her bony frame (so says the boy's older brother), which emanates sadness. And fear. Yes, fear! She flinches when someone's desk flap slams shut. She's wearing big sunglasses today, even though it's such a dark winter. But it doesn't matter, anyway, she's about to turn around any moment now, her chin juts out sharply again, now she is looking right through the class, with or without the glasses that conceal her, and several kids start to feel a knot in their stomachs. A year seven girl passed out in front of the blackboard last year. She had fallen face down on the brown wooden floor without the slightest warning, like a fascist struck down by a bullet in a film.

Once, the boy had set off towards home from school, along the motorway. On that occasion, the bus did not arrive, and some children from their village decided to walk home. It was spring, the footpath was still yellow from flowering coltsfoot. Yes, that was a long time ago, perhaps even in primary school, when the school had not yet turned into a dark and narrow endless tunnel, where you could not raise your head, you could not escape. Even before they had reached the large cattle barns, one of the fathers, driving his UAZ,[25] turned around with a bold curve on the dirt road, and then drove all the children home one by one. Maybe it was the teacher of the after-school care group who had called his workshop from the school phone.

The lofty pink sky of the morning had now dropped low and was ready to change. The boy pushed over the frozen furrows and felt the sweat on his head under his beanie. The field was harder to cross than he had expected. The forest on the other side of the frozen waves of the sea of snow shaped by the night wind was slowly coming closer. The thick, fluffy snow had a delicate cover, which had fallen this winter and stayed through December, long before the New Year, when it tended to penetrate one's boots as the feet sank in the ground with every few steps. With a ruddy face, he stopped and stuffed a handful of clean snow into his mouth. Then, panting, he looked back toward the centre of the cluster of buildings. The school grounds and the warehouses towering next to it had already shrunk to a small size, the trees and houses had become fuzzy dark shapes whose only purpose seemed to be to separate the greying sky from the snow-covered ground. Ahead, the sharp firs of the dark forest rose from the mist, an old road winding between the trees. The teacher marked the boy's absence with a line in the class record when the boy stepped under the tall spruce trees. The road had recently been cleared of snow. After wading through the snowy fields, it was nice and easy to tread here. For a while, the boy could walk through the forest like this. Walls of snow rose up to the waist on both sides of the road.

The spruce tree forest ended, and there followed eight-hundred metres of open space, on one side were forest meadows and a crumbling barn, on the other a clearing, where brown raspberry stalks pierced the snow, as summer adders slept in burrows underground. A narrow lane of linden trees led to the cottage. Behind the tall spruce hedge was a narrow potato field, a strip of meadow, then the mixed forest began.

The snow on and around the roadside milk stand had been trampled, the boy sat on the stand for a while and rested. In the surrounding snow, there were rings of milk jugs and traces of wellies, and for the first time today, the boy felt the cold, the cool air touched the boy's slender legs through the coarse blue fabric of his school uniform trousers. Let Mum say what she wants, but long johns are not the kind of clothing any sane boy would wear when entering the PE changing room at school. After PE, there is a lunch break. The boy did not have a watch of his own, but the place suggested that the bespectacled caretaker would soon ring the lunch hour. The smells of food waft into the classrooms on the second floor, followed by running, cold water and crowding into the windowless washroom in the basement covered with pale blue tiles. On Mondays, it is usually pea soup, but the one-pot meal or the curved smoked sausages in a warm white sauce, served with blue potatoes, are better. It had been a while since their class last had a stint at potato peeling. You are not permitted to leave any eyes in the tubers thrown into the great tin tub, but they still boil blue. In autumn, all the older classes are in the potato field, the boy's mother provides cotton gloves and veterinary rubber gloves to put over them. Mum has small hands. How do those women manage, whose hands will not fit in a three-litre jar, Mum says with carefree sympathy as she pushes blackcurrant leaves and long dill stalks onto cucumbers in the jar. And furthermore, no one is making mushrooms this autumn. The boy's hands don't get cold in the field, but in wet soil the gloves of the other children begin to wear thin as soon as they have started digging in their first furrow. Last autumn, the rains came early. The field was split into sections, the children were divided into pairs, everyone was given boxes and buckets, and the tractor loosening the potatoes kept pacing back and forth. If you harvested quickly, you could sit on the boxes and have a potato war with your neighbours. Some pairs at the end of the field ran into real puddles with their boxes, their wellies got stuck in the mud, drizzle turned into rain and chaos began, crawling around in the liquified mud, making out like they were looking for potatoes. The fields are long, the teachers cannot get everywhere. Potatoes and rocks started flying. Wet soil was in the children's gumboots and covered their knees and sleeves in a thick layer. The calls of the teacher could not be heard over the little tractor. On the way back, some had to stand, soil and mud spread on the bus floor for miles. If he had those blue potatoes now, the boy would eat them.

A wind predicting thawing weather had begun to swirl

in the tips of the spruce trees, the boy knew that tomorrow the snow would fall from the top of the branches in noisy chunks, leaving the wet branches swaying wickedly and darkly. But before the thaw, there must be a blizzard and… the boy recalled why he was on his way, and a cold knife of pain flashed between his heart and rumbling stomach. The Russian language caused difficulties for many in the class, not only for the boy. Thanks to his older brother, the boy read fluently even before he started school, and when different, boxy letters came in the first year, he remembered them easily. And their old teacher was very calm too. A slow walker, and a slow talker. With a grey head. Not at all like… Larissa. An evil, cruel rat. This winter's snow is so high that it would even penetrate Dad's thick felt hunting boots.

The food is, of course, real pig swill. What's worse is that I am the only Estonian here now.

If sometimes, while waiting for a children's film on a Sunday morning, the boy left Central Television's 'I Serve the Soviet Union' playing, his mother would turn the TV off when she walked through the living room. The boy had already realised that his childish hope, to see his brother appear on the flickering screen, a semi-automatic around his neck, his Pilotka military cap[26] casually resting on the back of his head, elbowing his way among the other soldier boys, winking at the boy with a familiar grin through the kinescope and thousands of kilometres away, was somehow not to his mother's liking. The boy knew very well that there had been no letter from his brother for almost three months. He himself visited the post box at the Mihkelson road junction several times, and saw how his mother became smaller each time when the boy returned panting with nothing but a bundle of newspapers under his arm. There is more to do in the army than writing letters, the boy tried to comfort his mother. The mother answered the boy only with a look, a dark flash of anguish for the boy's naivety and pity for both of their fears and longings. But this was only the blink of an eye in a long day. The next moment, his mother was normal, packing elbow-length plastic gloves and giant syringes into a grey leather bag and driving to the barns to inseminate cows. The boy stayed home alone to remember his brother's sending off, his brother's look, when he unexpectedly, painfully grabbed the boy's shoulder before getting into the car, looked at him with his face almost touching the boy's, looked right through him, like a gypsy reading a palm, or like someone looking into a mirror when they are alone.

There is a lot of ignorance here.

In the long northern winter, the night warns of its coming. It is a silent and luminous, imperceptible, and fleeting hour of mercy. The dull shadows and grey of the trees lie timidly in the forest meadow, and a crack in the grey, snow-filled sky flashes pink. Roe deer, whose delicate feet dig through the crust of snow in search of food at the edge of the forest, flare their nostrils and raise their heads restlessly in turn. Then one of the herd cannot handle the excitement, and the fragile silhouettes move, throwing snow dust high into the air. Hunting stands tower over meadows and fields like sentinels. At the edge of the forest, where badger setts have formed mounds under the trees and the pungent stench of game penetrates through the layer of thorns and snow to the surface, there is a line of human tracks. The boy's step is more uncertain now, as if his mind is losing its confidence. The cold stalks the defenceless in the forest and has already marked the stray. For an hour and a half, the boy has kept his course away from the path that leads to the forestry centre but has postponed stepping off the logging track until dusk. The eyes must adjust, and soon the forest wanderer will have nothing left but to obey his tired and hungry body and allow the snow and the winter night to carry out his plan. The traveller is whipped by the creeping wind, which promises snow as it rises. The boy already feels the cold, large snowflakes on his rough cheeks.

How are you doing there yourselves? My homesickness is terrible...

Even the longest school day comes to an end, the noise from the cloakroom lockers dissipates and in the glare of the swinging electric light, the cleaner wraps a crumpled grey rag around a long brush. A green sports bag with a worn bottom makes its way from the corner of the corridor to the caretaker's desk, along with a lone glove and crumpled neckerchiefs from the girls' changing room. Walking towards the apartment buildings in the shadow of thuja hedges, the caretaker looks up to see the stars, but the first soft snowflakes of the night fall on her face. She thinks about distant galaxies and the infinity of the universe, everything that is written about in Horizon magazine. In the barn of the collective farm, the boy's mother holds the calf hanging from the cow by the legs and turns it inside the body of the large animal, with the strength of a trained veterinarian, gently so as not to hurt the animal, and thinks of her eldest son, who still does not write from a faraway country, from a frozen desert, from a lonely spaceport in the middle of an endless desolate place. Not from Afghanistan though. Not from Afghanistan, the mother finds herself wondering, repeating out loud, what luck, what happiness, the cow with its pink tongue licking her calf panting from the long birth. The aroma of the fresh straw, the bloody foetal sack and the farmy smells make the mother's head spin, she kneels at the cow's feet and wants to fall into the night of the wet calf's black eyes.

There isn't much difference from prison here.

When that boy was found by the ditch and word reached the school, its icy core touching the children and adults alike, their mother said that freezing is the best death. It is cold at first, but then it gets warm, then very warm, and then you fall asleep. The three of them sat on the sofa, the mother spoke, in a low, somniferous tone, with soothing foreign words, hyperthermia and lethargy, and at the same time she kept stroking and stroking her sons' hair, this petting was even a bit funny, but they let her. The hay in the roe deer pen is crumbling, brown, but still smelling of summer. The boy squeezes through the half-rotten, fragile sticks of the feeding tray, pulls his knees under his chin and piles hay on top of his feet. This should take a little more time. The boy is in no hurry, but the cold stings his bitterly tired toes. The grey blanket of twilight moves into the manger and turns it to black. The boy's slim body trembles slightly in the deer hay, and the cold tends to feed doubt. What class might have been cancelled today? Maybe Larissa got so badly bruised from her stupid PE teacher over the weekend that she is sitting at home with a sick note and wearing dark glasses. But what would that change? The school is still a prison and there are too many years ahead. When it ends here, it will begin again elsewhere. Russian language teachers, fists, stones, spit, and the boys' toilets, where recess can last for days, they are the same everywhere. The boy claws and licks the salt rock brought to the deer with his tongue. A cold stone of pain.

Any word from Dad? Will he come back home?

The boy's father was away during the summer months of this year, he was involved in military exercises as a driver, hauling radioactive sludge to its burial site that entire hot summer. When requests started to come to the men at the workshop, one after another, his mother did not allow anyone to open the door when knocking was heard, neither the father nor the boy. While the mother was making her usual rounds in the barn on a warm April evening, the father and the boy were sitting in the dark room, behind brownish-red woollen curtains, watching TV, the film was *The Hound of the Baskervilles*. His father's summons was waiting for him the next day in the office of the collective farm, and he did not see the end of the film, the second part. The boy saw the eerie glow of the dog's phosphorescent jaws in his dreams, even in the autumn. Dad said that it was filmed in Estonia, those bogs and parks.[27]

Going to the forest, where his father went that summer, was strictly forbidden. Dad said so when he still lived at home. When he came back from there. While he was still speaking with them. Barbed wire surrounded the forest. Those who dared to go closer could see the tops of trees scorched as if by an invisible flame. And the silence! There is never silence in an Estonian forest. The forest is alive, breathing and stirring, the birdsong does not stop even at night, the animals move and make noises, their bodies brush against the branches, the trees groan as their bark tightens when they grow. The silence of the forest there had terrified Dad and the other men. This had been a silent, stagnant summer. The birds were either dead or left the forest. To go to the forest was to go to death. After hearing about this, the boy dreamed that he was walking in a forest of windless, voiceless silence, where the only sound was the rhythm of his heartbeat on drumskins, and in every direction he tried to look, stood a row of trees with yellow tops. And he knew, knew without seeing, that there lurked the glowing, radiant beast of the Baskervilles, right behind the trees.

Sometimes I think I dreamed of going to university.

The veterinary car was still parked in front of the barn late in the evening, fresh snow covered the Niva in a soft layer.[28] A yellow light sneered at the snow from one of the windows of the long dark building. Reclining in a brown armchair with torn covers on the armrests, the vet saw her husband under closed lids, wearing a radiation suit. Men in radiation suits and men in tin coffins had started to appear in the dreams of the boy's mother since the departure of her older son, and the return then leaving again of her husband. A tin wall now stood between her and her husband. The mother knew that she could not penetrate the heavy tin, of her husband's belief that death had travelled with him from there, and that it was the husband's duty to build an impenetrable wall between his wife and death. The tin is between a person and death. The boy's mother cannot even dream of going through it, just as one woman had had the tin coffin of her son who had hanged himself while doing his military service unwelded, despite it being prohibited. Weak, couldn't handle the pressure, that's what the stamped papers said. A familiar body with a battered face was lying in the tin box, a rope twisted into a tie was set around the neck. The boy's mother screamed hoarsely, helplessly through her sleep, and the smell of instant coffee and the ringing of the phone entered her mind at the same moment. The night watchman lifted a pipe with one hand, and with the other passed the vet a steaming cup, made of porcelain from the Estonian Age, and fringed with a faded gilt rim.[29]

The cold rustled in the hay, and the boy was troubled by the thought of his mother, who still meets him at the bus stop with a kicksled, when the weather is bitterly windy or when the stars were plentiful and predicted cold nights. The boy keeps saying that she would not come, that the path is not long, he is not small any more. Others see that. The edge of the ditch is already yellowing from coltsfoot, the cool spring weather is still taking its toll, but the boy is now on his way home. He is not alone beside the ditch, another boy, who is in full winter clothes, a fur coat and a striped beanie knitted in a cooperative, is walking in front of him. The boy starts walking after the other, quickening his pace to catch up. He wants to ask why he is wearing winter clothes in the middle of spring, but the distance between the boys doesn't get any smaller. They walk like this for a while, the boy is already getting warmer from walking. Then the unfamiliar boy turns, and suddenly it is his brother. The same co-operative tasselled beanie, which is now too small even for the boy, is again on his brother's head. Why don't you write, the boy asks. The brother smiles, then the unfamiliar boy laughs, from a distance his mother approaches in the Finnish sled, it's hard to breathe and the spring sun shines directly into the boy's eyes.

Later on, I will probably cross out some of the sentences I'm writing, Mum. I am actually writing this letter from the hospital. Sometimes things happen... that don't need to be written about. Or do they? No. Don't you worry. There is no need to worry. The food is better here, and you can sleep. And think, even think too much.

Mum, do you still remember that boy who froze to death in our neck of the woods? Who got off the bus in the wrong place. There is no way to go AWOL from the unit here, because... there is nowhere to go. In winter, the surroundings are an endless and boundless snowy desert. Anyone who dares leave would meet a similar fate. Why am I feeling guilty when I didn't even know that boy? I lie here wondering how this could have happened...

The schoolboy falls asleep on the bus on the way home. The road is long, the school day is long. The bus hums, and the cabin is warm from the long journey, the winter weather is gloomy when the buses reach the outskirts. The child wakes too late, his stop has been passed. He grabs his school bag from the seat and pulls on his jacket sleeves as he reaches the bus driver, frightened and sleepy. The driver stops and presses the switch, the doors of the LAZ open with a reluctant sigh, the icy air from outside pushes into the bus. The bus driver looks away, looks to the left. As now the boy climbs down, stumbles, the bus driver looks at the white and glittering snow in the dark field in the headlight, the snowflakes flying into the cabin. The stinky diesel cloud dissipates slowly in the cold, and the darkness of winter rolls down the road from the rear lights of the bus, the absolute total darkness of remote places. The boy begins to tread back along his well-travelled path, into the black and white night...

Now get ready to laugh, Mum! While I'm lying here killing time, the army is hard at work. My comrades, hard-working Soviet conscripts from distant fraternal republics, are *currently whitening the snow. They whitewash the snow, just like we whitewash a wall at home. Yes, you read that right! In the eyes of power, it is suitable to see only whiter than white. And why not whiten it. If you can. You wouldn't want to step barefoot in the snow around these barracks either. Because it's black snow, smeared with all that slush and soot as soon as it falls on the ground, all that reeking fuel spilling all over the ground. From shit. From mazut.[30] It's stained, the wrong colour snow. This snow would be too ugly for you.*

Life, like in a Film

Lilli Luuk

He said your life is like in a film.

After I went downstairs, when I stepped back onto the street, I started to think. I guess so. My life, like in a film. At times. But what is the film?

When I was still a kid, we lived like we were in an Estonian children's film with lots of sisters and brothers, playing circle games in a farmyard.[31] Only, we started in this film from the ending. The farm and the meadow, the garden and the potato field, which bloomed in the heart of summer, that was the beginning. There were many children, not as many as in the film, but we numbered five in the end, and we ran around in the big garden where the lilacs stood behind the table, the beehives situated beside the field. Maybe we sang, too. Like in the film. Father certainly sang. But our father was not an actor. And we did not have a horse. It was my grandmother's house, but she died soon afterward. After that summer.

Those funerals were like a film. Dad cried in the cemetery and bent down on his knees to scrape up soil to throw on Grandma's coffin. The horns of the funeral orchestra glistened and shone in harmony with the yellow birch leaves. Eventually, it started to rain on that cold day, and our feet got wet between the graves. In the canteen, Dad sang again. We played on the cafeteria stairs for quite a long time. There was a cultural house opposite the canteen where films were shown. But only on Thursdays.

Grandma's old house burned down like in a film. When Dad fell asleep with a cigarette, it was a Priima, we had to run out of the house in the middle of a dream.[32] Dreams are also like films. Mum shouted and screeched outside, and kept counting us, but it turned out that Mum could no longer count to five. Between the two of them, the father of the neighbours' children and the policeman, they had to hold her back. The dwelling part of the long barn-farmhouse blazed fiercely, lighting up this vast shooting location as far as the village houses.[33] We stood barefoot in the snow like children from some historical film, and black and white flakes kept falling and falling from the sky.

The funerals were once more like a film. Mum could not bear to leave the cemetery, she just lay on top of the smaller mound, trying to cover it with her winter coat, her mittens, her fox collar and fur hat were filled with dirt and sand, and the bandsmen, with their shiny instruments, had to pull her off the earth in the end.

After the winter there was no house, no garden, father nor little brother. The apartment was narrow and hot, outside there were trees for beating carpets and a sandpit, where cats clawed nonstop. On some late summer evenings, we climbed an old tractor at the workshop, my mother sat in the cab, and we drove to pick up apples in the moonlight at some abandoned farms, sweet summer apples, yellow transparent and then pippins. The light and scents in these night gardens were remembered like a film.

When the police were called to collect my stepfather, in the barn where my mother worked, we saw blue flashes and heard sirens like the effects in a film. My stepfather had an axe, but my mother's face was bloody and blue only because of his fists, since my stepfather was strong like a movie hero and my mother was nimble like a stuntwoman. When my stepfather came back from the sobering-up cell, he shared his love for my mother with passion like in a film. Children should not be allowed to watch these kinds of films.

At school, we had to be all for one and one for all, as in the Musketeers film.[34] I had to fight often. The maths teacher also started harrying me because whether it was the basement or the second-level stairway, it was not quiet enough for learning. Sometimes we didn't learn at all, but just sat inside a cupboard. There was always something going on in our home, like an adventure movie.

My mum once came to school, a bit like the mother in the film about the orphanage that screened in the same year, she asked me to return the school lunch money she had given me that morning, but unfortunately, I had already handed it to the teacher.[35]

My big brother soon ran away from home, as often happens in films. He was arrested and put into the cage of a striped police car. Soon he wrote to me about the army, that real war was not like in films. In the meantime, I was beginning to like Janek, one of the characters in the film *Four Tank-Men and a Dog*.[36] One day, a letter was written to my mother saying that my brother was a hero, serving his country like that show on Central Television. His coffin was flown back to Estonia and was never opened here again.

The summer after my brother's funeral, we moved to a new place. Moving made the impression of being like a film because we moved at night. My little sisters' dolls were left behind, as was my new brother's cot, my mother threw our things straight into the boot of the car and when my stepfather rushed out the hallway of the apartment building with an axe, the tyres of the Zhiguli squealed like in a chase movie and stepfather ran after the car like in a very romantic film.[37] That old apartment building had furnaces for heat, not radiators.

In the new place, I got to know this one boy. Our first kiss on the school dancefloor, behind the heavy curtains in the hall, was like in a film, with a soundtrack. That whole year at the new school was like a teen romance. At that school, the teachers did not bother anyone. In the summer, we would dive and swim in an old sand quarry full of water, and I soon learned that when someone drowned, they drowned very quietly and unnoticeably, not with their hands splashing water everywhere and screaming for help, like in films.

Funerals are always like a film.

In autumn, another boy, whose name coincidentally was Janek, said you have breasts like Vera.[38] At the end of winter,

I started vomiting in the morning, just like in the very same film. Before my mother understood what was going on, spring was over and we were able to race around the village roads properly with the boy in his Sierra, this boy who was already working in the sawmill. On the trail between the fields, there was a protected glacial boulder positioned behind a sharp curve, and a great pile of stones lay waiting for the passengers in the back seat, and I can testify to the fact that the statement that your entire life flashes before your eyes at just such a moment, as in a film, is absolutely true.

The baby survived, I did not give up the child, I fought for him and against everything, like in a film.

When I went to night school, life seemed to take a good, lively turn, and sometimes I felt like I was living in a film. My grades at night school were very good, my first year at university was sound. Weddings were like those in films, a church and a mansion. There was no need to go back to school, no need to go to work, there was a lot of money like in the movies, but love was like a fairy tale. I counted up to three children, and soon I was a sponge in my husband's house, where my mother's face looked back at me from every mirror. Life was now like my mother's favourite series, but I couldn't tell her that, nor the journalist who interviewed us, who let me cover up with make-up on, and put the picture on the cover of a magazine. I would have bought a rope, but I didn't have my own money.

Blue Beard had money, but in one year it no longer had any value, he couldn't afford the rope himself, and he had to start the Lexus behind a locked garage door.

The funeral was modest.

I went back to live with Mum, back to my neighbourhood, like a heroine returns in some films. Mum and I comforted each other, shared our troubles, we'd had a hard life, not like in a film. There was nowhere else to go. Life was now moving fast like a tape in an old VCR. Love came and went so much faster. I noticed that the shots tended to repeat, and soon I was counting to five. Teachers began to harass the children at school, soon I became acquainted with a municipal social worker, the constable himself was looking for an introduction. One foggy autumn morning, I woke up and couldn't count to five any more. I wanted to jump out of the window like in a film, but my mother's flat was on the ground floor. The other four were taken away as well, I screamed at the window of the ground floor, cars with different flashing lights drove into the driveway and out of the driveway, and the people from the flats talked later in the village and to the evening paper and the report, about how everything had happened as in a film.

It has become like a black and white film.

I do not remember my mother's funeral, as if I had fallen asleep before the end of the film. After my mother's flat was expropriated, I live in the city, not in a film, but in a jungle. Here I share my life, my pilfering and territory with people, most of whom have lived like in the film.

When he interviewed me for his film, he said I was very lucky. This film will soon be shown at large, international festivals. Usually, people of my social status are not so lucky to get into a film. Even if you have lived like in a film.

I still didn't go to School then

Aliis Aalmann

I still didn't go to school then. At that time, when the birds gathered the wind in their wings and took to the skies in the autumn. I tilted my head back and counted the bellies of the geese, and in the morning, I woke to the crowing of the neighbours' rooster to go and see if frost was on the ground. It was. It covered the grass and the dogs' muddy tracks. The frost had spread to the flower bed where tulips and primrose had grown in the summer. Grandma had said there would be snow when the swans migrated, but our pond still had swans and I didn't expect snow. I was looking forward to going to school. I was hoping that I could grow a little taller, so that I could reach up and peek into the neighbours' garden without having to stand on tiptoe, when I grow taller and get my school uniform, and then I will be allowed to wander into the woods. They wouldn't let me go alone. Last winter, Jaagup had disappeared while crossing the railroad tracks on his own. He had a forest hut. He had put the planks together himself, covering them with branches. A hiding place in a willow thicket, where he played with the boys, that they were soldiers, protecting freedom. They had taken a picture with Grandpa's old camera and promised among themselves that they wouldn't tell anyone, but word got out and not everybody was impressed. That the boys are playing war. Imagining themselves as great liberators. That they are waiting for when they can get their hands on some real guns with real bullets. 'Who will they shoot first?' was the question on quivering lips. 'Who last?' Because that was important, too. The last one had to suffer the greatest fear, trembling that soon it would come to him too. The older generation knew how to talk. They were familiar with it. I didn't know it yet, but I learned from them. I wondered for whom I might be the last. I said it once too. I whispered quietly to my mother and burst out laughing with excitement because I had thought of an answer.

But Mum shook her head. 'That's not right,' she said. 'You shouldn't be imagining that at all.' She added something about summoning the devil. Once a wolf attacked a neighbour's sheep. Dragged its bloody corpse across the field. Mum said that's why she did not want sheep. Said her heart could not handle it. Only chickens, a cow and two pigs—they were enough. I was taught how to take care of them. However, the birds were the loveliest. Those who flap their wings and squawk loudly, I am as one with them. And while the boys were playing at using sticks as weapons, I was gathering mossy branches to mix up an imaginary soup in puddles, using leaves, slicks of oil and dead flies. I had invisible animals to feed with soup. I treated their sickness and rabies. I believed that my broth would heal the world. In the meantime, I waved the stick about to round up the chickens. Part of me, just a small part, wanted to imagine myself in the boys' gang. That if they had guns, I could lead the troops. The chickens were my soldiers.

I still didn't go to school then. Jaagup was already going, and he disappeared. He still did not have enough wisdom to stop him himself venturing into the woods over the railway, where the branches didn't just snap off the slender legs of animals, but those of others too. Who knows what creatures crawl about in there. I was not told about the monsters who skulked beneath the spruces. Instead, I was told to look at the fading flowers and think about how time goes around in circles, at one point you are at the beginning of the circle, though not as you were before, slightly different. And that meant that time was over. 'That is why the trees have annual rings,' Grandma said, tracing a line with her finger around a birch stump, which had still provided sap in the spring. But now the tree had begun to loom over the house, and it had to be taken down. 'Dangers must be removed,' said Grandma, and I believed her, nodding along. 'Dangers that are dear to the heart, too.' I did not understand the second point because I still didn't go to school then, but I believed that once I finally stepped with my own patent leather shoes into that bleak, noisy little schoolhouse, I would be able to learn what such confusing sentences meant, which seemed to signify a lot more to grown-ups than to children. Or maybe the grown-ups had forgotten how to say things simply. Maybe there is a complexity to growing up that one cannot escape.

After Jaagup disappeared, the adults were worried. They did not know who or what might be prowling about the woods, but something had happened. Something that had to be kept a secret. This was evident when the friendship group broke up. The boys who had been hanging out on the street stopped looking at each other, and when I asked Hannes what had happened, he mustered up some phlegm and spat right on the footpath. He blinked with his honey-brown eyes and shook his head. I promised myself at that moment that I would never gather up stones again. You never know who has spat on them before, and how could I appreciate a rock with dried-up snot on it. 'You're asking too much,' he said.

'I want to know.'

'It's none of your business,' he said, adjusting his hat. 'Why do you need to know? You're just a little snot-nosed kid.'

My eyebrows furrowed as I stared at the stone. In the past, the neighbourhood boys had hurled demeaning words at me, like 'shrimp' and 'snot-nosed kid', but I did not understand why. After all, I had not bothered them, yet they considered it necessary to hurt me. At that time, I was too taciturn to say something back to them. Rather, my ears sank like a dog's, and I wandered over to where my mother's floral dress came into view, and that made the boys laugh that I was now, tail between my legs, under someone's protective wing, seeking comfort. I just stood by her side, while Mum fed the pigs or plucked weeds from the garden. 'Why are you following me around like a pet?' she asked me kindly, but she didn't look at me or see the tears in my eyes.

I mean, I wanted the boys to like me so badly so I could get in on their game, but they would not include me. They were fooling around and called me a rotten egg during the game, from whom they had to run away. They said I'm sick. They said that I'm infectious. They said I'm putrid. So putrid that I'm not even fit to play the rotten egg game. No matter how I tried to catch them, no matter how much I suspended the mixing of my healing soup, no matter how much I didn't slurp it, they were still fast enough to run away. That's why I wanted to get big. To finally catch them. To be accepted in the game at last. One day I had to be more than a snot-nosed kid.

'I'm looking forward to growing up,' I said quietly, tugging at the hole in the bottom of my shirt. My finger went through the hole. I twisted the clothing until it was tight. The finger coloured purple and tingled. I was staring at a lump of skin that was threatening to burst. But then I got scared I was going to lose my finger. I let go of the shirt.

'What, you'll grow up?' Mum marvelled. I realised she was joking, but at that point she seemed just like those boys. I was afraid that if Mum should think about the game, I wouldn't get to take part in it. 'You will always be our little nipper. My lovely little nipper.'

I wanted to spit. I wanted to spit right there, be it on the pigs, on the weeds, or right on Mum's dress. But I swallowed the mucus. I swallowed the sadness. It sank into the deep well of my soul and spoke the language of dripping water. There's not much air in the well, and I could hear how sorrow breathed deeply. Breathing like every breath would be the last, and yet it didn't die away. I wanted to grow up to go into the woods alone and find Jaagup's hiding place. I wanted to know what was going on in the woods. What the grown-ups didn't want to tell me. For once, I wanted to be braver than Hannes and the others.

2

I still didn't go to school then, when I caught Pille kissing Vasse behind the shed. I did not understand why she did it. In the case of a fever, Mum would press her lips against my forehead, but Pille had pressed her mouth directly against Vasse's. I couldn't understand why. Did they both have a fever? I knew we had a jar of Iceland moss on the shelf, but would that help them?[39]

They didn't see me. I was like a shadow. Like Grandma's cat, Miisu, who wasn't often seen, but she was always around.[40] She made his presence known by bringing mouse carcasses to the door and letting the dogs play with them. It was interesting to think whose door Jaagup had been taken to, and if anyone was playing with him.

I was sitting on the stone steps and Miisu came over. She pushed her head against my forearm, then slinked between my body and my arm, her tail upright. I patted her and sighed. That summer I fell down, injuring both my knees. I came home miserable and muddy. Grandma tugged at my hair, what was I thinking, running through puddles and hurting myself. Mum took my face between her hands and sighed:

'At least you're fine.' The kitchen smelled strongly of white onions, and I could not figure out if that was why my mother's eyes were red and wet, or if I should feel bad. It stung where Mum had touched my knee. The onion juice from her hands mingled with my blood. And when I drew my finger over the wound and tasted it with my tongue, I could taste onion.

'What do you mean, fine? The child is almost a cripple. She couldn't keep up with others before, now it's even more tragic.' Grandma pushed me into a chair, slapped down a bowl of soup and told me to eat. I ate quickly, my stomach growled so much. I ate so fast that even my sadness lacked the breathing room to get back on its feet. I knew why they were angry. I knew very well that they had thought about Jaagup's fate and feared that the same could happen to me. But I was not a mouse like Jaagup, I was a cat. In those moments when the other children didn't include me in their games, I watched Miisu's movements and became wise. I still didn't go to school then, but I was getting a little smarter. Miisu knew exactly where to find mice. Now I knew, too.

I was no longer frightened when my mother took a mug out of the cupboard, which held a dead baby mouse. I did not scream. Miisu had trained me, and now I knew how death came. It comes quietly. Even a rustling cannot be heard. It comes in so fast you don't even know it's already in the house. And when death is thrown out of the house, it isn't such a big deal. I could see why Jaagup had gone the way he had. I realised that death is not even talked about, even when it's shown. It is shown at a funeral. We went straight to the cemetery and in a row filed past the other graves. Some of the iron crosses had fallen over, some of the graves were overgrown with grass, and it was clear that no one cared for the person resting there. My toes were freezing. I especially remember that. The wind even whooshed up under my hat and whistled in my ears. I had stamped my feet and argued that I didn't want to put a woollen jumper on. I had run away from Mum, and she had given up. Now I was cold. I slumped my head over and kept it there, wiping my nose with my glove, not daring to ask for a handkerchief. Just kept wiping my nose, and the adults could see that I am one of those snot-nosed kids. I imagined how they whispered afterwards. How they downed their vodka and murmured about what a little brat I am. How I am sure to have the same fate as Jaagup, purely because I am so naive and stupid. Think about it, I didn't even put on a jumper, and with such a wind! Heaven help me! But nobody said it directly. Instead, they patted my shoulder and walked in silence. Rather, they looked down at me and pursed their lips together, so it seemed like they were smiling. The wells of our souls dripped to the same rhythm. I heard their sadness in their breathing. But in the end, they drowned their sadness with their shot glasses. I was even more miserable. I heard the sadness in the wailing, but it couldn't get out of the well.

I grabbed a sandwich from the table, pushed the sprat with my finger onto Mum's plate, and chomped away at what was left. The taste of sprat was still tingling on my tongue. It was tingling so hard because I knew how much Jaagup enjoyed sprat sandwiches. In his day, sandwich in hand, he had run away from me. He had teased that he would be full, but I would have to starve until Mum got home. Grandma would shake her fist at the door, what are you playing at, boy? I had wanted to laugh but had not been able to because I didn't know who was talking more seriously out of the two of them. I probably cocked my head and mistrusted them both. I suppose I thought I wasn't going to start eating sprat sandwiches, I'd sooner starve. Now I think differently.

'My hands are shaking so much,' Grandma said at the time. 'Wait, my chickadee, until Mum comes back.'

I nodded and wondered whether Jaagup was a chickadee too. He ran as fast as the sparrow flies. But then he stopped at the garage, sank to his knees, and probably coughed. Perhaps his stomach started to turn, and he vomited the sprat sandwich somewhere in the bush, and that could have happened too. He didn't fly far. Jaagup's flight stopped short. Jaagup's flight was extinguished in the woods, and so far, the truth was unknown. Sometimes it seemed to me that the shadows must have known.

When I looked at the coffin at the funeral, Jaagup wasn't there. It was a rag doll wearing Jaagup's clothes, with a face drawn on it. There, on the motionless chest of the doll, were white flowers. Much whiter than the doll's own skin.

'This is not Jaagup,' I said firmly, and Grandma smacked the back of my head. Grandpa's disheartened gaze stared back at her. My head began to hurt, and I still couldn't understand why she had behaved like this. I thought maybe somebody was making a cruel joke, but Jaagup wasn't anywhere. And when I got home, he wasn't there either.

Mum was sitting at the table, her cheeks flushed, her eyes narrowed. Grandma looked different too. She took the shawl off her head and let her hand fall on the table with a bang. 'There are no words,' she said quietly, and Mum nodded.

The mewing of a cat could be heard outside, and I ran to the door to let Miisu in. Her paws left muddy prints on the floor. Eventually, she jumped on the kitchen table, right on Grandma's beautiful shawl. Then Grandma yelled, 'Always this damn cat!' And Miisu was frightened. I left the adults to be sad, and found the cat. I climbed under the bed next to Miisu. When I exhaled, the balls of dust scurried away from me. They looked like feeble baby mice. Miisu thought it wiser not to catch them. I watched her and learned.

3

When a new item came into the shop, Grandma was the first to paint her lips red and grab her bag. She said to me quite seriously, 'Now let's go quickly to buy some sausage.'[41]

I knew it would be hard to keep up with her, but I tied a scarf to my hair and painted my lips red, which Grandma then wiped off and rubbed with water by the bucket. Her hands were sinewy and rough, and smelled like potato peels. They smelled earthy. 'Where do you think you're off to that you need to beautify yourself? You are still a child.' And I was. I still didn't go to school. I did not know how to get to the shop. I made a mental note that no one except Grandma could paint her lips to stand in the queue for sausage. Some things are simply forbidden to children.

Grandma made her way to the front and called after me. I thought it would be wiser to wait halfway, otherwise I would not be able to walk back. But no, she waited for me, grabbed my arm and just pulled me along. The dust blew wildly off the footpath, I remember. The birds were already singing. I didn't know the others, but a great tit sounding the alarm *tea-cher tea-cher*. Every time I had heard *tea-cher tea-cher* in my short life, they were stacked together, forming a chorus. A nostalgic cacophony, that I had reluctantly grown to love. After winter, any sign of spring was like a gift.

It hadn't rained for several days, but the mud reeked of spring. I liked the smell. I promptly drew in several deep breaths and sighed loudly. Grandma didn't like that. She was in a hurry. She needed to get to the shop first, although she could already see that we were not the first. But Grandma's hope wasn't dashed.

'We'll get there,' she said firmly, urging us on with a nod. 'We won't go without. I've let myself be trodden over so many times in my life, that... Oh, why am I rambling to you. But kindness can still be rewarded. If there's a God left in this world...' Grandma wasn't a believer. Yet she couldn't think of a better name for the one she would turn to from time to time.

Vasse rode his bike on the other side of the street. He had recently painted it green, a proper pine colour. Now, he was waving, and I was waving back, but Grandma didn't like that.

'I'm not convinced by these boys,' Grandma grumbled. 'You know what'll happen to him? He'll probably go to work on the railways like his father.'

'My father was on the railways,' I said.

Grandma yanked me harder. My legs buckled and I tripped, but Grandma was so strong that she kept me upright. 'Come, come. Unlike others, your father is a good man. At least he doesn't drink. That is why he left. The others drank so much that they sullied the earth.' I tripped again. 'Look where you're going, too.'

And I looked, but I no longer saw what was happening around me. I looked so intently and counted the pavestones. I imagined that each one had dried-up snot on it, but I couldn't tell whether it was Hannes' or someone else's. Nor did I notice that Hannes was strolling beside us on our way back home, and brushed against my shoulder. I was so afraid that Grandma would be annoyed by my slow pace, that I carefully considered my pace, maintaining my speed, and didn't see Hannes trudging along with his hat. I only heard someone spit behind my back and closed my eyes for a moment. Yet another paving smeared with gob. I shuddered with horror. When I got home, I hurled the stones outside, even the one that Jaagup had once given me. I threw it particularly far because what if Jaagup had spat on it before giving it to me, then laughed behind my back. Maybe all the boys had laughed and called me 'snot-nosed kid' since then.

4

I do not remember exactly how Blackie died, but I still didn't go to school then. It was spring and the ditch was filled with water. Blackie lay on her side, anemones all around in bloom, the wind whirling the dried leaves to shreds and through my hair. I stood back a little, my eyes watering. I watched her, my hands hanging down, and I did not know what to do at first. If tears fell, it was only because the spring wind was so strong that it actually tore water from the corner of my eye.

Blackie was a nice cow. Black and white spots. She liked to have her nose patted and would push her nose into the palm of your hand and draw her tongue over your fingers. Her black coat was smooth and soft, and she gave good milk. A rich milk that was good to swig directly from the milk pail, even though Mum and Grandma didn't like it, but sometimes they did it too, and apologised to me.

I think Blackie was Grandma's favourite. Grandma hugged Blackie a lot more than me, but I didn't mind. I thought it was nice that someone cared so much about Blackie. All at once, Blackie was on the ground, stiff and hard. Flies had circled around her before, but now there were more of them.

There were so many of them that I didn't even venture to drive them away. I just stood back and watched, not daring to make a sound or run home to tell Grandma what had happened. I think Grandma would have been annoyed. Not because I had done anything wrong, but that I had lingered so long. In fact, she had given me the task of feeding the chickens, but I had walked off. I wanted to see how much water was in the ditch. I wanted to jump in with my wellies and splash water around. I wanted to pick anemones. I wanted to mix leaf soup with a branch. And that's how I discovered Blackie too.

I was wondering who would provide our milk. I thought that now I would have to eat dry semolina pudding, and I would not like it.

Hannes clomped along beside the railway. His hat fell off, right onto the brown autumn leaves that emerged from under the thawing snow. Hannes shook the hat dry and put it back on his head, his nose a little wrinkled because now the wet hat was on his head. He froze when he noticed me. There were more voices from behind. Vasse and Rihhard were there too. They were poking and pulling at each other.

'Well, what have we here?' Rihhard enquired, and instantly collided with Vasse, who looked for the support of a tree trunk.

Rihhard leaned forward and laughed, hands on his knees. 'You little witch,' he said. 'Now you've cursed the cow, huh?''

I blinked at them. The wind had blown away my tears. My eyes were dry.

'A dead cow!' Vasse said in astonishment and clapped his hands.

'Goddamn snot-nosed kid,' Rihhard shook his head. 'Has

she turned into a witch?'

'Where have you been, anyway?' I asked angrily. 'You're not allowed to cross the railway.'

'Or she will forbid it!' laughed Rihhard. 'You're just jealous that no one takes a little kid along. Jaagup didn't take you, and we won't either.'

'Let's go,' Hannes said. 'There's no point with her.'

'A snot-nosed kid and a witch,' Rihhard said cuttingly. 'Who are you going to curse next?'

'Maybe you'll get cursed?' Vasse suggested.

'Or you, if you're keep talking so much.' Rihhard put his foot in front of Vasse, but Vasse clung on to him and didn't trip. They shoved each other and started walking.

Hannes slipped his hands into his pockets and stepped closer. 'But seriously, what did you do to that cow? Jealous, were you?'

I shook my head. 'Why are you so mean?'

'We're not mean, we're honest,' Rihhard corrected. 'Honesty's a virtue, snot-nosed. Not that you would know that. Your mouth is full of smoke. I've seen it. It's like a steam engine.'

'Like old Ülo's chimney, when it heats up the sauna!' Vasse laughed. He didn't know that I had seen them. That I knew his and Pille's secret.

'Then you know what happened?'

Vasse lowered his gaze and patted Rihhard on his shoulder. They seemed so stupid. How had Jaagup wanted to be their friend at all?

Instead, Hannes was the one who replied, 'You ask too much.' But this time he didn't add 'snot-nosed kid'. This time it seemed that Hannes was holding back. I did not know why.

When the boys walked from the garden fence to the street, I was still standing by Blackie and looking at the railway. From there, they had come across the tracks. From there, they had appeared between the woods and on to the meadows. This meant that the hiding place was still there. This meant that they still went there but had not told the adults. This meant that I was the only one besides the boys themselves who knew their secret.

I finally said it. I told Grandma that Blackie was no more. She nodded and hugged me. 'So much death,' she whispered. 'And you had to see it. Goodness me.' In the evening, Dad went with the neighbours to take Blackie away. No one wanted to leave her to rot beside the ditch. Besides, it would attract wild animals, and we had chickens to protect from foxes, and dogs that were too small to repel a wolf.

Grandma and I wove a delicate wreath from the early spring flowers to put on the grave, even though I suspected that Blackie was not buried there. It was too small for the layer of soil. I suspected that the grave had been dug to placate Grandma and me. I assumed it, even though I didn't go to school then. But there are things that you can't learn at school.

5

I was sitting on the stairs, a garland of dandelions circled about my head. I was afraid that ants had gone into my hair, and I scratched anxiously, but that summer the mosquitoes were even worse. Even when they were half-defective, they could suck your blood and make your skin itch. Grandma dabbed the bumps with vodka and comforted me by saying that at least the birds could eat.

'And fly away in autumn?' I asked.

Grandma nodded. 'Mosquitoes are also necessary, even if they harry us. And what does it mean if a mosquito wants to suck your blood?'

'That your blood is good,' I replied.

'Healthy. Exactly. The blood of a healthy person. Mosquitos are not fools.'

I wanted to ask so much, but I didn't dare. I wanted to ask what happened to Jaagup, but I wasn't sure if the adults even knew. I wanted to say that Hannes and the boys probably knew, but they lied. Instead, I remained silent. Instead, I used my fingertips to make rings around my mosquito bumps, and wondered how you might count the years of a person. Are there circles somewhere? It's hard with wrinkles. I had tried. I'd counted all the women's wrinkles, but I still couldn't tell their ages. I had craned to look in the mirror to see if I had wrinkles on my skin, but there were none. It was only when I raised my eyebrows that folds appeared on my forehead. But it was the wrong number.

Now I was sitting on the stairs, looking down the straight street, at the end of which was the shop where Grandma and I went from time to time. It was not visible from here because the horizon curved. Besides, the street was dusty. But Grandma said it was going to rain in the evening and then there would be no more mosquitoes.

'Why do you say that?'

She shrugged. 'It's a feeling. My left knee aches.'

'But mine doesn't ache,' I said thoughtfully.

'You are not as weather sensitive as old people.'

'But when will I know?'

Grandma patted me on the back and smiled. 'There is time, chickadee. You don't want to grow up so quickly.' I didn't understand why.

Miisu snuck up in the distance, a motionless mouse in his jaws. Her tail was proudly erect as she walked across the garden beds and masterfully onto the stairs, jumping right beside me. The mouse was laid on my lap.

I looked at that grey character. I started to feel sad. I couldn't do anything for the mouse. It looked so sweet and miserable. I didn't even dare give him to the dogs to play with, even though they would certainly have wanted it. Miisu pushed her head against my hand and purred quietly. I turned up the edges of my skirt and walked behind the shed where there was loose soil. Mum wanted to make a garden bed there. In the very same spot where Pille had given Vasse a kiss. And in that same place, I buried the mouse that Miisu had caught. I dug a hole with my hands and slipped the mouse in from the edge of my skirt. The grey body fell into a hole with a quiet bump. I pushed it into the soil and levelled it nicely. It is possible that the dogs unearthed it later. It is possible therefore that they played with him. However, I had done my best. I took the garland from my head and placed it on the grave. I knew Miisu was not at fault. Cats do catch mice, and that was the reason we had her. But it was a pity, nonetheless. I wonder if Jaagup had been caught by someone who did not know any better. Like Miisu. I wonder if he took Jaagup to someone's stairs to show off. A tear came to my eye over the mouse. I felt like Miisu couldn't be otherwise. And then I remembered that I hadn't cried over Jaagup. I tried. I tried to squeeze tears from my eyes, but as soon as I thought about Jaagup, I became numb. The streams of tears dried. Behind the eyes there was a desert.

☪

From time to time, I dreamed of school. For example, when I dangled on Dad's knee. But lately, there was a fear in my soul that Jaagup, with flaming eyes, would crawl out from under the sofa, and would no longer be himself. And he comes to me to complain that I haven't cried for him yet. He asks, even demands, why I have begun to forget. I was afraid that teddy bears were hanged with the same black funeral ribbons and dragged behind him. Just like those empty boxes of sprats that time when a bridal party drove past the house. I looked out the window. I stood on tiptoes and pressed my round potato nose against the glass, straight onto black fly dung, which I hadn't seen. Outside the window, a spider swung from its web. The wind did not blow him about. Instead, it blew a drowsy fly into the web. It stayed there, buzzing. It was left begging for help. It was calling to God. I only heard the boxes of sprats, not prayers. I heard the noise of engines and squeals of delight. I saw the bride's white veil waving out of the car window, fluttering like a sheet, only more effortlessly and more beautifully. I was so jealous. I was so positively jealous that I quickly jumped off my chair, my nose a little tender, and ran to pull Grandma's apron.

'Make it for me too!' I demanded. 'Make me a veil. I want to get married too!'

My grandmother's wrinkled face looked at me kindly. She had just been knitting and rubbed her throbbing hands.

'And to whom should we marry you?'

'Whoever would like to. I want to wear a veil!' I said with

determination and stomped my foot on the ground, as I had seen my father do. 'I also want the veil to flutter in the wind.'

Grandma did. The old dusty silk curtain was gathered and run up quickly. She made several knots to prevent the thread from breaking. Although she told me that I shouldn't get the curtain grubby, she knew in her heart that the white curtain, which was already tinged with grey, would eventually end up muddy or stuck someplace. But she enjoyed my happiness. She enjoyed the little girl shining brightly, and not thinking about the dark side of life.

I attached the veil to my hair with clips and twirled out of the door like a cloud. But gently. Just as gently as dandelion seeds fall when they are blown from a stem. I sashayed over the stone stairway and floated down the steps. The chickens clucked, reproving me. The pig lifted his snout from the trough and looked at me with his small currant eyes. A crow flew overhead, in such contrast to my white veil. So magical. I waved and danced. The wind slinked into the silk pattern, whirling and whistling in my ears. The veil was like long hair. The veil was lightness, though it was a bit heavy, and finally my head started to ache.

I hadn't seen anything else from the window except the veil's beautiful patterns. Grandma had seen something else. It reminded her of Pops, and thought that even though love was beautiful, it was painful too. Out of this, Mum was born, frizzy-haired, soot-marked, and flour-dusted, but what scars Grandma carried on her stomach. When we went to the sauna, I saw them. I didn't dare to ask, but I thought I had seen similar trails spread out in the sky. It happens when a plane leaves white strips, like when a plough draws furrows in a potato field. But what's growing in the trails of airplanes? What is growing in Grandma's stomach?

Nonetheless, the anxiety vanished. It was swept away by my soaring white veil. For a moment.

7

A plane flew over the house. It left white stripes like a cat's milky whiskers. Mum obtained milk from an acquaintance, but Dad already knew someone who was willing to sell us a new cow. Grandma suggested that I could think of the name, but I looked from the window to the railway and didn't listen. The branches moved. Someone was walking over there. I quickly slurped up the last of my soup, even though Grandma forbade me from eating quickly. You have to enjoy a meal. But the bowl was empty, the picture appeared at the bottom—a wee boat on light blue waves—and I already said my thanks.[42] I slipped my feet into my shoes and ran outside. The sun shone. I had to shield my eyes with my hand to see better. Until now, I hadn't encountered the boys to follow them into the woods. Now there was hope. Now they seemed to have forgotten to keep their bigger secret. Now my legs seemed fast enough to catch up with them.

Rihhard was the last and loudest in the line. He seemed to seek out all the branches and step on them. Hannes was in front and couldn't tell him off, but Vasse turned around and hissed at him. I had to take cover behind the trees so they wouldn't see me. I had to think silently like Miisu, silent like a mouse. I imagined myself transparent, like a lace curtain.

'Can't you be any quieter?' Vasse bristled. 'If someone is nearby, they will hear us a kilometre away. You're like a tank steamrolling everything.'

'Tanks are powerful,' said Rihhard, and shoved branches out of the way, bending down a little. 'Are you saying I'm powerful? Maybe if you didn't tell me off so much, the group would be quieter. Even wild animals scrabble about as they walk.'

'You can't stay silent for any length of time.'

Hannes had already moved ahead of them, I couldn't see him any more. Hannes was earnest and quiet. Hannes was reminiscent of Jaagup. Maybe that's why I was seeking his attention. I lingered near him so that he would notice me, even if only to call me 'snot-nosed kid'.

Overhead, a crow cawed, and somewhere further away the tapping of a woodpecker could be heard. I got tangled in a spiderweb and almost screamed. I rubbed my face to get rid of the tingling feeling. A pinecone dropped nearby, and it startled me, but the boys were far away. I accelerated my pace, keeping low. In one place I stepped into a stream because I had never been here before.

It was my first time alone over the railway. Cold water taught one to tread carefully. Experience taught what the eyes could not. Dad still liked to say that a person rarely learns from the mistakes of others, but also not from their own.

I knew I had to track the boys several more times and mark the trail before I dared to go alone to their hiding place. I had ribbons at home to tie to the branches. But I had to tie them so that the boys wouldn't notice. When my mother asked, I lied. This was probably the first time I had quite intentionally lied. I said mice had taken the ribbons. I remembered that this was said to be so. If the mice could pinch a dummy, why could they not take ribbons? Mum pursed her lips, and I knew she did not believe it, but she did not say anything. Perhaps she realised that lying is sometimes useful.

The next day I went with new ribbons and tied them in such a way that only I could see them. So that I could find the way to the hiding place and back. And so far, I crouched in the shade of a spruce tree, watching the boys. How did they carry planks from one place to another. How did they bang a way with a hammer, with such serious faces.

And then finally, when the boys had just returned, I was still waiting. I waited for them not to return. I waited for no one else to emerge from the bushes.

The woods were quiet. The wind rustled and the birds sang. I heard insects prying away at the tree bark. Perhaps it was a wasp somewhere in search of material for a nest. I had heard at home about how wasps nibbled and pecked, demolishing a roof beam, or chewing at a plank of timber, from which yellowish colour flaked off. I carefully stepped out from the cover of the spruce branches and entered the hut where the boys liked to go and whatever they had just been working on. I did not understand the attraction. A shack. A cubby house. My arms were covered in goosebumps, and I shuddered, but I did not give up. Sometimes fear is a friend because it warns of real horror. Fear is what makes you seek safety. Yet this time I didn't listen. In fear, I wanted to draw into the background and wait. I stepped over rags. There were books on the ground, some properly stacked, the backs facing upwards, others were scattered, their pages lolling out like tongues. Some were like a stomach turned inside out, the content in one place, the covers in another. Did the boys go here to read in secret? Did they dare not admit that they might have actually liked something that's compulsory at school?

I studied the walls and the ceiling. Dark shadows flourished there. Shadows and mould. The damp of winter had found itself a nest here and tasted bitter in my throat. A delicate light penetrated through the cracks, directing the rays in a criss-crossed pattern in the shack's interior. Crooked nails were hooks for toy guns. I carefully touched one of the guns with my fingertip and although I knew it wouldn't go bang, I pulled my hand away. I walked like a cat around hot porridge, glancing here and there. It was forbidden. I had been warned about this. 'Don't play war,' Grandma used to say. 'Do not summon evil.' One of the nails was bare. I took a step closer and raised my hand to touch it, but I didn't dare. A free nail, as though for me, but the boys hadn't included me in their play. I was left out. I felt jealous. Not that I would have wanted to play war, but I could have managed running with the boys through the fields of hay. I could have at least held a wooden gun in my hand and raised it triumphantly into the air. I could have joked around with them. I would even have agreed to bring sandwiches along as a thank you if I had been accepted by them. One nail was bare, but why? Had it belonged to Jaagup? Had he owned several guns? Was it for someone new? If the boys were to accept Pille in their gang, I would never forgive them. I'd rather they call me 'snot-nosed kid' for the rest of my life than see anyone else in their games.

I squatted on the floor and touched books. Dusty and mouldy. Rough. Moist. I looked at the names and titles written on their spines, none of them seemed familiar. Or maybe one that had once been on Grandpa's bookshelf. But now Grandpa was no more. Hadn't been for years. I only remembered his rough hands. They smelled of engine oil and smoke.

The floor was covered with thin wooden tiles and the wind was blowing underneath, that was how I heard it, even though I knew that wind didn't live underground. I shifted the books and tiles aside and stared into this gaping void in the middle of the hut. Like a chest without a heart. Cold and darkness was blowing there. It was a mouth that wanted to swallow. I was like a fly before a web. The slightest breeze could have pushed me closer to my doom. I knew I couldn't fall properly. My father had told me that many times. 'You're falling the wrong way! You're falling like you're going to hurt yourself.' But I couldn't teach my body. It didn't listen to a word. Or did I use the wrong words? I didn't dare tell Mum about the falls. Recently, she had started crying from pain, and when my father happened to see it, he became angry. 'Who has ever been healed by tears? Have you? Me?'

'These are my tears,' Mum replied, facing Dad with watery eyes. 'Please.' But what she asked for, I didn't understand. I only saw that my father sighed and stepped away.

Now I took a step closer to the brink, but I couldn't see what lay below. The light beams broke off at the edges. The darkness cut them off. There was a ladder against the wall. I dragged it closer and pushed it over the edge. The legs of the ladder rested on the bottom; the upper part stuck out of the hole. Fear awaited me on the brink. I nodded and started to climb down the ladder. The wood groaned under the weight of my body.

The darkness heard me falling into it. It was quiet, didn't say hello. It didn't nod. I stepped down from the last rung and listened, will the floor fall away, will I keep my footing? I swayed onto my feet, my knees limp from the test. Nothing happened, but I felt like someone was watching me. My eyes adjusted to the dark. I swallowed. The ensuing sound echoed far beyond me. It meant that the room was bigger. I walked carefully on the dark sand, groping about with my hands so that I wouldn't bump into anything. I could see a glimmer. Someone had tried to dig a tunnel, and a tunnel had evolved, at the end of which was a glow. But the light was so faint, that at first, I couldn't tell who or what was making it. He was huddled there, his head sunk forward, his hands muddy. Jaagup. And sorrow was fastened around his waist. I blinked, and then my shoulders sank. And the corners of my mouth turned down. I blinked. I put one hand against the wall, just in case, and held onto a ladder rung with the other. At that moment, the thought flashed through my mind, if I fall now, will I be able to fall properly? Would Dad be proud of me?

The sadness caressed Jaagup's curly, sandy hair, which stuck to the sweat on his forehead. Jaagup sighed. He had heard me coming, but couldn't look at me, he just kept cowering. We were silent for a while. I kept blinking. I stared once at the sadness, once at Jaagup. How could he be here? How could they both be here?

'I dig, but I can't get out,' he said at last. His voice did not echo, but it reverberated through me, because I was hollow inside. As I looked around, I realised we were in a well. It was an old well that no longer held water. And someone had poured sand in to fill it up.

'But where have you been?'

Jaagup swayed from side to side, like a tree branch swinging in the wind. Except that there was no wind here.

'Somewhere in the middle,' he replied. 'I heard them calling out to me in the woods. There was a commotion of voices, and I just kept digging, but I could not climb out of here.'

'Why didn't you call out?' I asked.

Jaagup sputtered. 'What would I shout with a mouth full of sand?'

I swallowed.

'I heard voices, but not you, not the boys,' Jaagup admitted.

'Who then?'

'Pops. Even Helgi would cry in distress.' He shook his head. 'Pops would have said, you got what you wanted. Pops would have slapped me on the back of the head,' he said, his face twitching in ghostly pain. 'Pops would have known that I myself was to blame. We were told. They all said, don't...'

I vaguely recalled that at Jaagup's funeral, I had noticed a small tombstone in the cemetery. But I couldn't read.

'Are Mum and Dad mad?' he asked.

He wiped his fingers against his jacket. For a moment, it seemed that Jaagup disappeared completely into the darkness. He would be like an illusion, from his familiar surroundings, flown into reality and could no longer cope here. The magic of the fantasy had disappeared.

I had to look away because I think I understand. I saw the sand, I saw something sticking out, but I squeezed my eyes shut quickly. Sadness unhooked itself from Jaagup and creeped closer, I heard it. I took a step back, held the ladder more tightly. I still didn't go to school then, but I knew why the boys hadn't spoken, and why the adults didn't want to believe them. Now I had to be that same witch who mixes the antidote in rainy puddles. I imagined I had the magic words. I enchanted a heart as hard as stone, but sadness had already touched it. I had no choice but to climb out of the hole quickly. My glance through tears was misty, misty for the first time, I pushed the wooden tiles back into the well. I cast a glance at the nails for a moment, especially at that lonely, bare one, and then I walked home. My pockets filled with ribbons. It was so hard to keep walking while untying them from branches. The ribbons were like rocks. Sadness had caught me. It did not help to build a shack on top of it. It did not help to push the tiles into the big mouth of emptiness. It did not help to sneak in and mourn from time to time.

I did not speak of this to others. I told my mother that the mice brought the ribbons back. I did not go to the woods any more, because maybe someone would have seen, maybe someone would have followed.

I did not want them to know where sadness lives.

To the Moon

Aliis Aalmann

Eduard was a simple man. He loved simple things like the weather forecast and the evening news, walks in the misty city and vodka. All of them in moderation, not exaggerated. He also loved women. Some were just so beautiful that he could not help but fall in love with them. Some were clever, some wore airy dresses. Eduard liked things that were pleasing to the eye.

Liisa wore her hair loose or—when she was working—she tied a colourful scarf on her head. Eduard marvelled at the scarf's patterns, and sighed wistfully to himself. He would have liked to untie the scarf and loosen Liisa's dark hair. The temptation was great, but instead he fiddled with the bottom of his shirt, walked to the well and back, forgetting the bucket and the water completely.

He had to go back a second time, but he still forgot the water. Rather, he thought about how to pass closely by Liisa. The distance still seemed too great, insurmountable.

There was always some kind of gulf between them.

Liisa was simple. Eduard did not understand what he liked most about Liisa, either her simplicity or her beauty. Yet it is said that beauty is hidden in simplicity. So then, the first option was preferred. Liisa liked to plant flowers and pull weeds in garden beds. She had always considered that she had green fingers. Once, a bee stung her. Eduard saw it happen. Instead of leaving the bee where it lay, Liisa made a little grave for the fallen winged creature in a corner of the garden bed. She wiped her tears and asked forgiveness from the Heavenly Father that she had created a situation that caused the bee to sting her. She was so caught up in her own thoughts that she did not notice Eduard, who was looking solely at her from the well, an open secret admirer. Eduard worried that Liisa wouldn't notice him. The woman had admirers across the town, but none of them was exactly what the heart yearned for. One had a vodka problem, another a different habit, one who was unkept, another who was poor, arrogant, reckless, a scoundrel or just plain stupid. Eduard could count on the fingers of one hand some of his own flaws, but it was better not to think about that.

Even now, Eduard was watching the woman from the well. How Liisa stayed for a moment to admire her handiwork—gazing at the rows of flowers, head cocked, wiping the sweat from her forehead and finally standing up. Eduard flinched.

Liisa took a bag of soil and a shovel and placed them in the old shed. She threw her gloves on the wood pile, locking the door with a rusty padlock. The key squeaked in the keyhole, making Liisa recoil. Eduard took a step closer and right there his courage ended. He was too shy to continue. And just as suddenly as the courage had disappeared, the chance to talk to Liisa also disappeared. Liisa vanished too. She went into her flat, put the water on to boil for tea, washed her hands and started preparing dinner.

A despondent Eduard circled around the well, hauled a bucketful of water into his apartment and went to the bus stop to talk to Toomas. Toomas offered Eduard a plastic bottle of beer, but he shook his head.

'Not today. Today I need a clear head,' he replied nervously, and rubbed the palms of his hands on his trousers.

'And you don't drink beer at all,' Toomas muttered, shaking his head.

Eduard mumbled. 'I do, in company. But—but otherwise I'm not a drinker. I'm not.' He shook his head and laughed at himself.

'I'm not a drinker either,' Toomas said thoughtfully, a glazed looked in his eye, and sipped his beer. 'I'm just thirsty … all the time.'

*

Eduard thought at length about how to tell Liisa that he loves her. But thinking was of no use. He was still undecided and hesitant, especially since Svetlana next-door seemed to check him out from time to time. Maybe he loved Sveta instead?

And what did he want from these women anyway? Probably a housewife who would cook for him. After all, love comes via the stomach, and his stomach was always empty. Eduard understood Toomas' thirst, but certainly not Toomas himself. Currently, Eduard was taking his meals at the church. He did not believe in God. Instead, he believed in Liisa, who still had two more years of schooling than Eduard. However, this had to mean that Liisa was smart.

One must have faith in clever people.

Even when the clever ones lie, they do so at the right time, so it's very easy to believe them. Some people are too smart. For example, Rutt's granddaughter Loona, who said that love is more like chemicals. Eduard did not want to believe that this was an illusion. He wanted love to be as simple as one plus one... or the weather. Variable, perhaps, but very real. If it's stormy, you quarrel, if it's raining, you cry, if it's clear, then, well... clear!

Sveta was probably not as smart as Liisa. But then he hadn't talked much to Sveta. In the sense that Sveta did speak, but Eduard often could not answer or had forgotten to listen. Therefore, Eduard had not come to a firm conclusion as to whether Sveta was smart or not.

Eduard was not clever. He was dead sure of that. He didn't want to be smart, because wisdom is complicated. Stupidity is much easier, and it's simpler to maintain. Wisdom has to be looked after, forbidden and commanded, stupidity is simply that.

Eduard rocked an old toy back and forth on the table. He could not bear to throw it away. It was reminiscent of his childhood. People say that everything is easier in childhood.

Maybe that is why Eduard considered it so close to his soul.

He saw from the window that Liisa was going to hang her washing out. Eduard took a slug of cognac from a shot glass, scrunched his nose, thumped his chest and walked to the front door to wait. The nerves were there, his legs were starting to shake. It was hard to stay still, with that strong desire to shift closer to the shade of the clean washing. That's what he did.

The sheets were waving in the wind. Eduard was afraid that he would somehow sully the laundry. That he would accidentally brush against it or breathe on it in the wrong way.

Meanwhile, thoughts came to him; cowardly thoughts, that maybe he was always doing something wrong. However, those thoughts usually went away quickly. Life wanted to live. Time should be used meaningfully, not wasted on overthinking.

'Listen, Liisa,' Eduard began. But Liisa did not listen. Eduard's voice had failed him, the words had sounded too soft.

'Liisa,' he tried again.

Liisa raised an eyebrow and momentarily peeked over at Eduard. She waited for the man to speak. So far, she had hung her laundry on the line and pinned it with pegs.

Eduard laughed awkwardly. 'Such a funny story that I am in love with you now and—would you come and be my wife?' Liisa put her hand on her hip and sighed. 'Go to the moon,' she said dully.

'Yes-yes-yes, then you'll become my wife?"

'I will become your wife,' Liisa mumbled, her focus on the washing again. 'Yes, that's a joke I'd like to see.'

A glimmer of hope appeared in Eduard's eyes. 'You will become my wife'… he repeated and nodded. 'Yeah. Well, yeah. Why not?'

'Why not, why not,' said Liisa, shaking her head.

'You be careful. Too much romance is not good for the soul. It makes you tender, sick, and susceptible to sickness and foolishness.'

She lifted the wash basin onto her hip and walked past Edward towards her room. She disappeared behind the door.

Eduard sighed. His shoulders dropped.

Where to go from here? He wandered down the street and started to search. Initially, he didn't even know what he was looking for. Gradually, though, it became clear.

But not before he had booted a great quantity of stones with the toe of his shoe, with a grief-stricken mind and a pained heart. It seemed as if every stone was unaware of Eduard's next move. He himself finally became so sorry for the stones that he whispered his apologies to the cityscape.

Then he had a flash of inspiration.

Eduard started to collect bottles to take them to the returns centre. There's money to earn from this.

'I will go to the moon,' he reasoned. 'To the moon... after all, love sends a person to places they haven't been to before.'

Eduard had not roamed or travelled much. He was a homebody. He had been to Latvia a few times, on one occasion this happened by accident. He got lost in the forest, mushroom basket in hand, until finally he heard the roar of cars and arrived at a camping site, where a foreign language was spoken. The location of Estonia was clarified for him with the aid of hands and feet.

The older he got, the more he pondered the idea of travelling a little. Sometimes he'd take a longer route through the town to make it more exciting. If the same paths are always trodden, they will wear out. And the legs will tire too. Eduard recalled a philosopher once saying—or was it Toomas—that you cannot step into the same river twice. But you can't step with the same feet either.

Eduard found a total of seven bottles. He carried them home in his arms and promised that he would go searching again in the morning. Seven bottles are not sufficient to pay for dreams, but it is a good start.

His morning round earned him three euros, five in the afternoon. In the evening, he tried his luck again.

It was repeated like this for a whole week, but then he discovered that it was nice to sleep longer in the mornings, and similarly, to take naps in the afternoons, so that he could do longer rounds in the evenings.

After dinner, he disappeared in the dark streets and collected bottles in plastic bags and his rucksack. He took them to the returns centre and calculated how much money he had raised to date, and how much more he needed to accumulate.

At this rate, Liisa will not even begin to love him. More money is needed.

The idea came to him to ask good people for help. Eduard went to the door of the first house he encountered, introduced himself as a polite person, and modestly asked if he could take their accumulated bottles for himself.

'I need to earn more cash,' he explained. 'To propose to a woman.'

'Take it, take it!' the man nodded and pushed a bag of bottles over the doorway. 'Good luck, citizen!'

In the second place, the door was almost slammed in Eduard's face.

In the third, there was no one at home. In the fourth place, he only got a couple of bottles, in the fifth they laughed at him, in the sixth, they barked at him that Christian manners meant toiling at work and not bothering strangers—Eduard did not have time to explain that he is a Christian, goes to church to eat and all—the inhabitants of the seventh house were kind. At the eighth door they demanded that he bring back the returns money, and Eduard did so. But then the resident began to accuse Eduard of stealing because he was sure there had been more recyclables.

'Half the cans were from Latvia,' Eduard explained, but he was not listened to. At this point, Eduard slunk away.

In the ninth place, an old woman thanked Eduard for his kindness and industriousness. In the tenth, there was interest in the man's motive.

'What are you going to do with these bottles?'

'I'll take them away,' Eduard replied with a broad smile.

'This will only make a tiny amount,' said the householder, shrugging his shoulders.

'I'm collecting. I won't waste it right away, I still have to behave sensibly.'

'A specific goal.'

'That's right,' Eduard said proudly. 'Liisa… that is, I told Liisa that I love her. She responded immediately, saying that I should go to the moon. Yes. I am collecting for that. To go to the moon. And when I return, Liisa will love me back. So, she said she'd like to see that. That is the joke. Well, that she and I will be together. That's how it is.'

The resident then began to feel sorry for him. He gave Eduard two plastic bags full of bottle returns plus a fiver for taking them away.

No one is safe from unrequited love.

'I wish you success in life. And in love,' the resident said.

'That success does come,' Eduard laughed. 'It comes to me and to you, lovely person. It comes to everyone!'

Eduard wished him a good evening and took the bottles to the returns centre.

There was still no money to reach the moon, but there was hope.

And if Liisa did not work out, Svetlana was also an option. I wonder where Sveta would send me. Later, he told Toomas the story, after which Toomas snorted beer up his nose and began to cough.

'You dear fellow,' Toomas said, and blew his nose onto the street. 'But think now, if Liisa had sent you to hell… you would have collected the money to get there, right?'

In Eduard's mind, this was not funny. His heart ached.

Translator's Notes

1—Johann Köler (1826-1899), Estonian artist and a leader of the Estonian national awakening movement of the 19th century, which campaigned for Estonian self-determination. Many of his paintings depict rural life in the late 19th century.

2—Timur: A reference to *Timur and his Squad* (1940), a children's novel by Russian writer Arkady Gaidar (1904-1941), telling the tale of a group of village children who secretly carry out good deeds.

3—*Romance of the Three Kingdoms*: 14th century Chinese historical novel attributed to Luo Guanzhong (c. 1330-1400, or c. 1280-1360).

4—*Genghis Khan*: 1939 novel by Soviet writer Vasily Yan

(1874-1954). *Genghis Khan* was the first in Yan's Mongol Invasion trilogy, followed by *Batu* (1942) and *To the Last Sea* (published posthumously in 1955).

5—Muhu: The third largest of Estonia's islands.

6—Juhan Smuul (1922-1971): Estonian writer, born in Muhu.

7—Saaremaa: The largest Estonian island, Saaremaa can be reached from Muhu via a causeway.

8—Merivälja: Estonian for 'sea field', Merivälja is a subdistrict of Pirita, a seaside suburb of Tallinn.

9—Juhal Smuul Museum: The Juhan Smuul Museum is now part of the Muhu Museum in Koguva on the island of Muhu.

10—Jaan Saul (1936-1966): Estonian actor.

11—Perioodika: In English, 'Periodicals', this Estonian publishing house existed from 1940-1941 and 1944-2002.

12—*The Land and the People*: *Maa ja rahvas* in Estonian, this 1959 novel by the Estonian writer Rudolf Sirge (1902-1970), deals with the events of 1940 and their impacts on Estonian village society.

13—Adventure stories from the land and the sea: *Seiklusjutte maalt ja merelt* is a series of adventure and science fiction novels for middle grade and young adult readers, published by the Estonian National Publishing House, 1955-1962.

14—Jaan Oks (1884-1918): Estonian writer and poet.

15—*The Library of Creation*: *Loomingu raamatukogu* in Estonian, is a book series published since 1957, which was created as a supplement to *Looming* (*Creation*) magazine. The books are published in paperback editions.

16—Debora Vaarandi (1916-2007), Estonian poet. Vaarandi was Juhan Smuul's second wife, marrying in 1952. Smuul was married to Vaarandi before he was romantically linked to Ellen Noot, the subject of this story.

17—Edgar Tõnurist (1920-1992): Estonian statesman during the Soviet occupation.

18—Urho Kaleva Kekkonen (1900-1986), Finnish politician, served as eighth and longest-serving President of Finland, 1956-1982.

19—Forest Cemetery: 'Metsakalmistu' in Estonian, the Forest Cemetery is located in Pirita, Tallinn. Many famous Estonians are interred there, including Juhan Smuul.

20—The restoration of Estonian independence occurred in 1991.

21—*Мыло*: Russian for 'soap'.

22—Hans von Risbiter: Character in the Soviet-era Estonian film *Viimne reliikvia* (*The Last Relic*). The film in set in 16th century Livonia. Made in 1969, the film was hugely successful and is considered a cult classic.

23—LAZ: The Lviv Automobile Factory was a major Soviet bus manufacturer based in Lviv, Ukraine. *Lvivskyi Avtobusnyi Zavod* ('Lviv Bus Factory') was usually abbreviated to the brand-name 'LAZ'.

24—A number of Estonian country schools use old manor houses as part of their school facilities.

25—UAZ: The UAZ-469 is an off-road military light utility vehicle.

26—Pilotka: a type of foldable military cap commonly used in the Soviet Army from the Second World War until the 1980s.

27—This is a reference to the Soviet film of the Arthur Conan Doyle novel *The Hound of the Baskervilles*, made for television in 1981, which used a number of Estonian filming locations.

28—The Niva is a type of off-road vehicle sold under the Lada brand.

29—Estonians often refer to the first Republic of Estonia, 1918-1940, as the 'Estonian age' (*eestiaegne*).

30—Mazut: a low quality, heavy fuel oil.

31—The author is referring to the classic Estonian film, *Nukitsamees* (English: *Bumpy*) (1981), directed by Helle Karis, and based on the children's story by Oskar Luts.

32—Priima: 'The Best' or 'Prime' in English, a type of unfiltered cigarette.

33—Traditional Estonian farmhouses sometimes had a barn at one end, and a dwelling part at the other. Sometimes the barn was made of stone, sometimes of wood, but the dwelling part was mostly wooden.

34—Reference to the Soviet film, *D'Artagnan and Three Musketeers* (Russian: *Д'Артаньян и три мушкетёра*), a three-part miniseries that first aired in 1978, and based on *The Three Musketeers* by Alexandre Dumas. The series was directed by Georgi Yungvald-Khilkevich and was extremely popular, shown often on television, and is now considered a classic. It includes scenes shot in Tallinn's Old Town.

35—The author is referencing *Naerata ometi* (English: *Smile at Last*) (1985), set largely in an orphanage. It was directed by Leida Laius and Arvo Iho, and was based on Silvia Rannamaa's novel *Kasuema* (*Stepmother*).

36—*Four Tank-Men and a Dog* (Polish: *Czterej pancerni i pies*; Estonian: *Neli tankisti ja koer*), Polish TV series made between 1966 and 1970, following the adventures of a tank crew in World War II.

37—Zhiguli: A type of car manufactured in the Soviet Union, based on the small family car, Fiat 124.

38—The author is referring to Russian film *Little Vera* (Russian: *Маленькая Вера*) (1988), which was very popular, and one of the first Soviet-era films to feature an explicit sexual scene. Vasili Pichul's film was shot in his hometown of Mariupol in Ukraine and takes a piercing look at the darkest recesses of everyday life in the Soviet Union. Much of Mariupol was destroyed by the Russian army during the Russian full-scale invasion of Ukraine in 2022.

39—In a number of cultures, Iceland moss is used in traditional medicine for various ailments, including colds.

40—Miisu: Common Estonian affectionate name for a cat. Equivalent to 'Pussy' in English.

41—During the Soviet occupation, certain foods were available in shops, but others, including sausage, were rare, which meant queuing was common.

42—In Estonia, diners—particularly children—traditionally say thanks (often 'Aitäh!') when finishing a meal, after which they rise from the table.